Susa ...
meet...
of Malta. ... met on
Monday, became engaged on Friday and married
th... mon...
and ...
and plays the piano, and when she's had enough of
relaxing she throws herself off mountains on skis or
gallops through the countryside singing loudly.

PREGNANT BY THE DESERT KING

SUSAN STEPHENS

MILLS & BOON

First Published in Great Britain 2018
by Mills & Boon, an imprint of HarperCollins*Publishers*
1 London Bridge Street, London, SE1 9GF

© 2018 Susan Stephens

ISBN: 978-0-263-93508-0

MIX
Paper from
responsible sources
FSC **FSC™ C007454**
www.fsc.org

This book is produced from independently certified FSC™ paper
to ensure responsible forest management.
For more information visit www.harpercollins.co.uk/green.

Printed and bound in Spain
by CPI, Barcelona

For my wonderful ever-expanding,
ever-supportive family.

PROLOGUE

Present day...

TADJ'S WORLD TILTED on its axis as a woman in a red dress stepped out of the kitchen.

'Excuse me, Your Excellency,' he said, startling his ambassador to London. 'Something extraordinary has just happened.'

'Of course, Your Majesty...' Raising his portly form as quickly as he could the ambassador bowed to his ruler and employer, the Emir of Qalala, as Tadj, an exceptionally striking-looking man, left the table where they'd been dining incognito, to stride across the floor.

Sensing his approach, the young woman turned and stared, paling, as if she'd seen a ghost.

CHAPTER ONE

Three months earlier...

A CASUAL COFFEE in the steamy café next door in her lunch break from work at the laundry had never involved plugging Lucy's body into a power source before. Lined up at the counter behind a red-hot Goliath with shoulders wide enough to hoist an ox, she reasoned it was only natural to be distracted, as her heart beat nineteen to the dozen. He was deeply tanned, with thick, inky-black hair that curled possessively over his neck in a way that made her fantasise about making it even more unruly; his short, rugged jacket might have been designed for no better purpose than to display his iron-hard butt, and long, lean legs. He was so big he achieved the impossible by making her feel dainty for the first time in her life. She was the woman targeted by slimming magazines who always planned to lose weight. And she would, just as soon as chocolate was written out of history.

'Would you like to go ahead of me?'

She almost fainted when he swung around.

'Are you speaking to me?' popped out of her mouth before her brain was in gear. Silly question, when the most devastating black stare was directed straight into her eyes. It was the most arousal-inducing stare she'd ever been subjected to. There were eyes of all description, some of them very beautiful, but these were astonishingly beautiful eyes.

'Can you move along, please? People are waiting to be served.'

Jerking alert as the lady behind the counter bellowed the instruction, Lucy shuffled along in line, and in doing so managed to stumble into Goliath.

'Perhaps you should sit down before you cause a pile-up,' he advised with amusement. His deep, husky voice with the intriguing accent, combined with his big, firm hands steadying her, blew her mind. 'Now?' he suggested as she stared at him transfixed. 'I'll get the drinks while you find the table.'

Finally, she came to. 'Do I know you?'

'I don't believe so,' he said, staring down from his great height. 'Coffee? Tea? Hot chocolate? Something to eat, perhaps?'

By now, people had turned to stare. One or two, having recognised Lucy, nodded and gave her a thumbs-up expression. She didn't want to make a fuss. This was her local greasy spoon. Nor did she want to bolt, giving the man the impression he intimidated her. Who was he? she wondered. There was only one way to find out. 'Coffee would be nice…thank you. Skimmed milk, two shots, please.'

As he turned to place their order she became aware of the buzz of interest in the café; most of it directed her way. Should she know him? Was he a celebrity? If only she paid more attention to the press. Maybe he had called in at the laundry while she was working in the back; no one could forget a face like that. He could pass for a sailor with his deep tan and super-fit appearance, but, with his commanding manner and expensive casual look, he didn't strike her as crew.

'When you're ready,' he prompted as he waited for their coffee to be prepared. 'The table,' he reminded her. 'There aren't many free. Better get moving.'

'Yes, sir,' she said, saluting ironically, but not before she'd absorbed his clean, spicy scent.

She did go to find a table, even though she wasn't a fan of domineering men. This man had redeemed himself with that curving, dark-eyed smile. She guessed he used it a lot, but this was a packed café, and not much could go wrong over a coffee. It wouldn't hurt to give him five minutes to see how he turned out. Her chums at the laundry were always complaining that nothing exciting ever happened, so at the least she'd be able to tell them about this when she got back to work.

She'd hidden herself away long enough.

As the unwanted thought shot into her mind, she shivered involuntarily, and recollections of her cruel, abusive stepfather came flooding back. Her mother's second husband headed up a criminal empire peopled by ruthless thugs. Thank goodness he was in prison where he belonged. Lucy had left home at her mother's insistence, to escape the increasingly unpleasant attention of her stepfather's henchmen. She'd been lucky enough to find genuine friends on King's Dock.

Having paused to acknowledge a couple of friends, she glanced at the man, only to see that he had not only paid for their drinks, but for an elderly couple's pot of tea. He'd be up a tree, saving a cat next, Lucy thought with a smile as he crossed the café towards her. She had to stop being so suspicious of men. They weren't all bad.

'Something wrong?' her new friend asked, frowning attractively as he drew near.

'Nothing,' she said, noticing how much attention he was getting. Both he and her stepfather were big, powerful men, but that was where the similarity ended. Her stepfather was a ruthless bully, and she could see nothing of the snake in this man. If eyes mirrored the soul she was safe; there was no evil in them.

Just heat, Lucy reflected with a bubble of excitement and amusement as he indicated that she should sit down. 'Or are you going to stand here all day, blocking the aisle?'

When he lifted one sweeping ebony brow like that, and smiled into her eyes, it was impossible not to respond. Her stepfather hadn't crushed her spirit yet.

'Are you going to join me?' she invited once she was settled.

She had to move the table to let him in. He was what might be referred to as a big unit, and she was hardly petite. And though he might be a player, and she his latest target, one cup of coffee did not a drama make. People knew her here, and she could leave any time she liked.

Today was turning out better than anticipated, Tadj concluded as he studied the lush-figured woman sitting opposite him. She had magnificent breasts, which even her bulky winter clothes couldn't hide. But it wasn't his automatic male assessment that struck him most, but her natural poise and unaffected manner. It was such a welcome change from the women who usually flocked around him, hoping for the position of wife, or mistress at the very least.

He'd been walking the dock, filling in time before a

party that evening on board his friend Sheikh Khalid's yacht, the *Sapphire*. Leaving behind the razzmatazz that went with the title Emir of Qalala, to mix with the crowds on the dock like any other visitor to the high-end marina, was a welcome release from the pressure of celebrity. Spending time with a woman who didn't appear to recognise him was a novelty. The fact that this woman probably wouldn't have cared less if she had known who he was was an unexpected bonus. He planned to stay on the *Sapphire* tonight, and a strange bed was always warmer with an agreeable companion at his side.

Or underneath him.

'Are you sure this is okay for you?' she asked, glancing around. 'You seem to be creating some interest. Should I know you?'

'You do now. And in answer to your question, this is perfect.'

'You didn't answer *my* question,' she pointed out.

'No. I didn't,' he agreed.

A tense, electric silence sprang between them. He'd sensed her before he'd spotted her in the café. His senses were always fine-tuned where women were concerned, but she had intrigued him from the first moment, with her elfin looks, and full, voluptuous figure. She wasn't remotely in awe of him, which only added to her allure. Half his size, she was quite a bit younger, though her character made up for any lack of experience.

'Good coffee?' she said, breaking the silence.

'Excellent,' he murmured, maintaining eye contact until she blushed.

In the course of his duties as ruler of one of the fabulously wealthy Sapphire States, he met many women, but never remembered them for long. None held such instant appeal. He weighed up her clothes and the body underneath. The cheap, unbuttoned coat was open over a clinging cotton sweater that spurred an urge to introduce her to fabrics that would caress her body. Kissing that challenging look off her face was another must, before bringing her to the heights of pleasure.

'You really didn't need to do this,' she said as he asked the waitress for a top-up.

'But I *really* want to,' he said, holding her stare.

'Do you always get what you want?'

'Most times,' he admitted.

He only had to raise a brow for her to read him easily. 'Lucy,' she said. 'Lucy Gillingham.'

The name meant nothing to him, but he made a mental note to ask his security team to check her out.

'Careful,' he said as she dipped her head to take a sip of the refreshed coffee. 'It's hot.'

'I'm always careful,' she said with a look that left him in no doubt she would never be a pushover.

The most astonishing jade-green eyes pierced his, tilted up at the outer corners. Lucy's expressive gaze was enhanced by a thick fringe of black lashes that added a feline touch to what was already a highly attractive package.

'Sorry,' she said, pulling back, and blushed attractively when their knees brushed.

'No problem,' he said, sliding his long legs between hers without touching her, but her blush deepened as if she was deeply conscious of the intimacy forced upon them by the narrow table. Colour tinted her Slavic cheekbones an attractive shade of rose. 'You have beautiful hair,' he said to distract her.

'And you have big feet,' she said, shuffling around to remove all chance of them touching.

Lucy wore her hair in a no-nonsense short, urchin-cut style. It suited her strong personality. In a rich shade of auburn, it reminded him of autumn on his English country estate when the leaves had turned from vibrant green to take on the tint of fire. She was fiery. She'd be amazing in bed.

'Oh, that's better,' she said, having drained the mug. 'I'm good for nothing before a coffee. How about you?'

'I'm good for some things,' he said.

Her cheeks burned red. He hadn't enjoyed himself so much in a long time.

How could talking about coffee be so dangerous? Lucy spent a lot of time daydreaming, but none of them turned out like this. If only she'd paid more attention to the press and laundry gossip, she might have a clue who the intriguing man was. 'You're new in port,' she prompted, waiting on more information.

'Another coffee?'

'Yes, please.' As he turned to speak to the waitress, her mind strayed to lazy days on a sugar-sand beach, with blocks of chilled chocolate at her side, and a bucket of lemon sorbet Bellinis to share with the mystery man as a prelude to very good sex, the details of which escaped her for now.

'Something wrong?' he queried as she frowned.

'Yes. As a matter of fact, there is. I told you my name. Or, do you have something to hide?'

He laughed and his entire face lit up. Attractive didn't even begin to describe the creases around his eyes and the flash of those strong white teeth. Raunchy? Her nipples were prickling without him even looking at them.

Close enough for her to detect his minty breath, and to register the fact that he didn't like shaving, he was an incredible lure with those incredible black eyes burning into hers.

'My name is Tadj.'

'Ah—like the Taj Mahal,' she said, relaxing.

'Tadj with a D,' he explained.

'Oh.' Her cheeks flamed up again. 'I suppose you hear that dozens of times.'

'Some,' he agreed.

The killer smile had returned to his face, but she settled for regarding him coolly. With his thick black hair curling wildly around cheekbones that would have sent Michelangelo crazy for his chisel, she guessed he must be used to admiration, and was determined not to add to it, though couldn't help herself wondering what that sharp black stubble would feel like if he rasped it very gently against her skin. Imagining her rounded curves accommodating his impressive hard-muscled frame led her to shift position on the bench seat.

'Tadj,' she repeated to distract herself fast. 'Nice.'

He was still staring at her with that faintly amused expression on his face, which led to one quick thought… melted chocolate, heated gently before being spread liberally over her naked body, for him to lick off. 'Okay, Tadj with a D, so now I know your name, but not your occupation.'

'That's right. You don't,' he said.

'Cagey,' she observed, narrowing her eyes. 'I'm genuinely curious.'

'And I'm genuinely cagey,' he countered with a scorching look.

They both laughed and the atmosphere lightened.

'So?' she prompted, coffee mug hovering in front of her lips.

'So, what? What do you want to know?'

'Let's start with everything?' she said.

'We don't have time.'

'Should I be worried that you're being so evasive?'

'Here?' He glanced around. 'Probably not.'

But later, she thought. She killed the thought as soon as it sprang into her head. There'd be no later. She'd try another tack to dig for information. 'So, what brings you to King's Dock?'

'Old friends and business,' he said.

'Intriguing.'

'Not really,' he admitted, sitting back. 'King's Dock is a convenient place to meet, that's all.' He raised a brow, as if challenging her to ask more questions.

'I must be keeping you from your friends,' she stated, reaching for her bag.

'You're not,' he said, still relaxed, still surveying her as a soft-pawed predator might observe his next meal.

As they stared at each other, a quiver of arousal tracked down her spine. He was enjoying this, she thought. And so was she. A lot more than was wise. Why had this extraordinary-looking man landed in the middle of an ordinary day? Time to take a tougher line. 'You sat me down, force-fed me coffee, so now you have to pay for the pleasure of my company with information.'

'You think?' Few women had ever made him laugh as Lucy did. Being so irreverent and funny was part of her charm. 'You won't get round me,' he warned when she pulled a mock-disappointed face.

'Why not?' she complained in the same style. 'Is what you do for a living classified information? Maybe you're a secret agent,' she speculated with a lift of her finely drawn brow.

'And maybe I'm a man drinking coffee in a café and minding his own business as best he can...'

'How boring. I prefer my version.'

'I'm in security,' he admitted finally. This was the truth. One of his many companies was responsible for the safety of some of the most prominent people on the planet. As the ruler of a country it was in his interest to hire the best.

'Aha.' Sitting back, Lucy appeared to relax. 'Now it makes sense.'

'What does?'

'Your evasiveness,' she explained. 'I'm guessing you handle security for one of the those big fat potentates on their big fat superyachts.' She angled her chin towards the window, beyond which a line of imposing vessels loomed like huge white ghosts against the steel-grey sky. 'What's it like working for the super-rich, mystery man?'

Her naivety was irresistible, but her innocence compelled him to tell the truth. 'Actually, I'm one of them.'

'A big, fat potentate?' she exclaimed, frowning in a way that made him laugh.

'I thought it was the yachts you thought big and fat.'

'You're being serious, aren't you?' she said in a very different tone.

'Your expression does my ego no good at all,' he admitted.

'Well, this changes things,' she said, 'and I can't help the way I look.'

'Having money changes your opinion of me?'

She hummed and frowned again. 'I don't have an opinion about you yet,' she admitted honestly. 'I don't know you well enough.'

He would be the first to admit he was touchy about money. His late uncle had plundered the Qalalan treasury, leaving it empty when Tadj inherited the throne. Tadj had built up a bankrupt country brick by brick. Even then, when everything was back on an even keel, a family to whose daughter he'd been engaged since his birth turned up to demand he marry the girl right away. It had cost him a king's ransom to sort that out. The experience had left him with a horror of state marriages, together with the distinct impression that a mistress was far preferable to a wife. He had to marry one day to provide Qalala with an heir as the constitution demanded, but not yet, and his thoughts regarding taking a mistress in the interim had just taken on a new and vigorous lease of life.

CHAPTER TWO

'IF YOU'VE MADE so much money out of the security business…' What was coming next, he wondered as Lucy gave him one of her wide-eyed cheeky, teasing looks. 'Can I ask you for a loan?'

He knew this was a joke, but bridled anyway at the possibility that she might be like all the rest. 'Ten pounds until pay day?' she pressed blithely, but she couldn't hold back the laughter, and, sitting back, she said, 'You should see your face.'

He adopted a stern look. 'You'll get away with that this time.'

'You mean there'll be a next time?' Quick as a whip, he thought as she added, 'That's assuming rather a lot, isn't it? How do you know I'll want to see you again?'

His groin tightened as he told her, 'Educated guess.'

Resting her chin on her hand, she stared at him in a way that made him wish he were clothed in flowing robes rather that snug-fitting jeans.

'Surely, you can run to a miserly ten pounds?' she pressed.

He reached for his wallet.

'Don't you dare,' she said.

'Can't I pay the bill for the extra coffee?'

'Touché,' she said. 'Just bear this in mind, Mr Security Man. I don't want your money. I don't want anyone's money. I'm doing fine as I am. Here—let me contribute. Save your money for your next coffee-shop adventure.'

'I doubt there'll be one.'

'Too much of a security risk for you to keep taking up with strangers?' she suggested.

'Something like that.' He stared at her intently, but there was no sign that she'd recognised him.

'I guess you have to be careful in the security business.'

'My involvement is in the security of a country,' he explained.

'Big stuff,' she said.

'You could say that.' He grinned.

'You must be pretty powerful. And yet you look so normal.'

He tried hard not to laugh. 'Why thank you.'

'Well, this has all been very nice.' She sighed as she gathered up her things. 'But now it's time for me to go. Some of us have to work,' she added.

'Let me walk you back—where do you work?' He wasn't ready to let her go.

'At Miss Francine's laundry,' she said with a touch of defiance.

He got it. Some of the rich yachties could be real snobs. If he turned out to be one of them, she'd rather know now. 'The laundry on the marina?' he prompted, having noticed the bustling establishment on his walk.

'Yes.' She pulled another of her comic faces. 'We've moved on from banging out dirt with stones at the stream.'

'Uh-huh. So, what's your job at the laundry?'

'Ironing and finishing.'

'You any good?'

'You bet I am.'

His lips twitched and then she laughed. It must have dawned on them both at the same moment that two strangers could share a table and chat over coffee, without things getting heavy.

'I'm sorry,' she said with a graceful flutter of her slender hands. 'I didn't mean to bite your head off. It's just that some visitors to King's Dock are snobby idiots and I wanted to be sure you weren't one of them.'

'I'd never have guessed,' he said dryly.

'So long as you're not a trust-fund yachtie with nothing better to do than spend your inherited money, I guess I'm okay with that.'

'Touchy about money?' he probed as they navigated their way out through the crowded café.

'Every sensible person cares about money,' she said.

'Well, I can reassure you on that score. Everything I've got I've earned. All I inherited was debt.'

'There must be something else wrong with you,' she said as they reached the door. 'No one's perfect.'

'Feel free to examine my faults,' he invited.

'Not likely! So, who left the debt?' she asked with her hand on the door. 'A close relative?'

'My uncle.' As he spoke and took over opening the door, he realised that he hadn't been this frank with anyone ever, let alone on such short acquaintance.

'So you repaid your uncle's debt as a matter of honour,' she guessed as they stepped out into icy air from the steaming warmth of the busy café.

He shrugged as he thought back to when Qalala's future had depended on a financial rescue package, and how lucky he was to have already made a fortune in tech. This had allowed him to vastly improve the lot of his people, and save the sapphire mines his uncle had been plundering for years.

'Let's just say my uncle almost ruined the family business,' he told her as they walked along.

'And you saved it,' she said confidently.

'You've got a lot of faith in a man you've only just met,' he commented.

Her extraordinary green eyes shot him a penetrating glance. 'I don't feel like this about everyone.'

For some strange reason, he felt the same, and wanted to tell her more about the history of his country, and how deeply he felt for Qalala. Meeting Lucy had turned out to be a real wake-up call. The type of wife his royal council was urging him to take would be a matter of business for both parties, whereas a mistress like Lucy would give as good as she got. 'So now you've got me all worked out, what's next for you?' he probed.

'I'd like to hear more about you,' she said.

'Some other time,' he proposed as they reached the marina.

'There you go again,' she said with an amused sideways look. 'That would mean seeing each other again,' she explained. 'So, where do you come from? You don't have an office pallor, so I'm guessing somewhere hot…'

'Somewhere far away,' he said.

'Come on, Mr Security Man. I need specifics.'

'So you can tell your friends?'

'Can't I be interested?'

Was he going to talk about the billions he'd made in tech? She'd run a mile. Lucy just wasn't the type to be impressed by money. And he wanted to keep her around a little longer. Should he tell her that he used to be known as the Playboy Prince, and his people, who had been downtrodden for years by his profligate uncle, hadn't expected anything of him? They couldn't have guessed that he'd been waiting for this chance to serve his country, and would seize the opportunity with both hands. Putting his business acumen to its most demanding test yet, he had transformed Qalala, and would continue to put the country before himself.

'And you accuse me of daydreaming,' Lucy accused.

He linked arms with her as they crossed the road. It was a gesture that came as naturally as breathing.

Tadj was gorgeous. And yes, she was smitten. She'd have to be a block of wood not to be affected by his firm touch on her arm, or those amazing eyes, scanning the street to make sure they were safe before he crossed. He was so rugged and tall and tanned, it felt amazing to be linking arms with him.

'Watch out,' he exclaimed as, distracted, she almost tripped over the kerb.

As his grip tightened and their faces came dangerously close, she determined to discover Tadj's true identity when she returned to the laundry. Someone was bound to know. Gossip was rife on King's Dock, and spread like wildfire. A man like Tadj would hardly go unnoticed. Her workmates would have all the juice, which would almost certainly include the fact that she'd been seen drinking coffee with him.

'I'm afraid this is where we part,' she said as they approached her workplace.

'Afraid? You?' he queried with a wry look. 'Those two things don't fit.'

'I'm not a thing,' she said, warming under his gaze. 'And I'm not afraid of you,' she added.

'I'm very pleased to hear it,' he said, making her a mock bow.

Everything about this encounter was new to her. She'd never had so much fun with a man. She'd never had fun at all. It was such a shame they would probably never meet again.

He frowned deeply. 'Do you have to go straight back to work?'

Her pulse raced. So he felt the connection too. 'Yes,' she said, instinct telling her not to make things too easy for him. 'Some other time, perhaps...'

'When?'

She hadn't expected him to be quite so direct. 'Soon,' she said airily as her heart tried to pound its way out of her chest. 'I'd like that,' she added honestly, feeling she'd been a bit harsh. 'And you don't have to walk me to the door.'

'But I insist,' he said.

'Do you always get your own way?'

'Always,' he said in a way that made a quiver of excitement tremble low in her belly and her nipples tighten to the point of pain.

'Thanks for the coffee,' she said when they reached the laundry.

'Just tell me one thing before you go,' he insisted.

She looked at his hand on her arm. He let her go. 'Okay,' she agreed.

'What would you do if you had all the money in the world?'

She didn't even have to think about it. 'I'd buy new machinery for Miss Francine's laundry and make sure she took a proper holiday. Did I say something funny?' She frowned.

'Only what I expected of you, I suppose.'

Lucy's heart pounded even faster as Tadj's magnificent shoulders eased in a casual shrug. 'Your wish is highly commendable,' he added, staring down at her with warmth and laughter in his eyes.

'But you're not the genie in the bottle,' she observed sensibly.

'I could be…'

'Not this time,' she said, warning him off with a mock-stern look.

As she was speaking, she was digging around in her shopper to find her purse.

'What are you doing?' he asked, frowning as she brought it out.

'Paying for my coffee,' she said. 'I don't like to be in debt to anyone—and you've had enough trouble, from what you've told me. I would have paid at the café, but you got in fast. Here. Take it,' she insisted, thrusting some cash towards him.

'I'll leave it as a tip for the wait staff when I walk past,' he agreed.

'Brownie points to you,' she said approvingly. 'Well, I can't be late for work.'

'Don't forget tonight—'

'Tonight?' she interrupted.

'When I see you again.'

'Oh, I don't know about that. I've got studying to do when I finish work.'

'Studying what?' he pressed, frowning.

'History of art. My dream is to be a curator, or a conservator one day,' she explained.

'Working in a museum or an art gallery?' he proposed.

'Exactly.'

Tadj stared at her long and hard. 'Anything else?' he said at last.

'I'll let you know if I think of something,' she promised cheekily with a glance inside the laundry.

'Don't let me keep you,' Tadj said dryly.

'I won't.'

'Just one thing,' he said.

'Which is?' she pressed.

'You'll need a party dress for tonight.'

'I've already told you, I'm not coming out tonight.'

'But you've got a party to go to.'

'No, I don't,' she argued, enjoying the game. How could she not, when Tadj's wicked black eyes were full of amusement?

'Yes, you do,' he insisted, acting stern.

'With you? Not likely!' she countered, wanting to prolong the moment of parting.

'On board the *Sapphire* tonight,' he tempted.

'You're kidding me! You know I can't resist an invitation like that.'

'Good.' His lips pressed down attractively, making her wonder what it would feel like if he kissed her. So much so, she almost missed his next statement. 'My friend Sheikh Khalid is having a party tonight, and you're invited as my guest.'

'That's news to me,' she said, heart pounding as she lifted her chin to confront those dangerous eyes.

'I can't think of anyone I'd rather take as my plus one. At least we'll have a laugh. What do you say?'

'Can't you find someone else to have a laugh with? Someone more suitable?' Lucy suggested, as the enormity of what she could be agreeing to struck home. A glamorous party on board a yacht that could slip its moorings at any point? However attractive she might find Tadj, or maybe because of it, her sensible self advised caution.

'I'm right out of amusing women at the moment,' he said with a somewhat cynical look that suggested this might actually be the case. 'And I don't relish being bored to tears by people trying to find out if the person they're talking to is as important as they are.'

'Good plan. But why me, when there must be dozens of better qualified companions?'

'Qualified in what way?' he demanded, pretending to be shocked.

'There must be dozens of people who'd love to go to that party.' *With you*, she left out, deciding that with his good looks Tadj probably didn't need his ego massaging.

'No one with your unique qualities,' he assured her, straight-faced.

She hummed and frowned. 'I'd love to know what they are.'

'That will become apparent as the evening goes on,' he promised.

'But as I'm not coming to the party…'

'Those unique qualities will force you to,' he insisted. 'You won't be able to resist.'

He might be right, Lucy concluded. 'Go on.'

'You work a real job, and meet real people on a daily basis. You're interested in everything and everyone, and you have your own quirky take on what you see.'

'You've gathered a lot about me in a very short time.'

He certainly had, Tadj thought. 'My point is you're real and I like that. You have no idea how rare that is.'

She thought about this for a moment. 'You make a very persuasive case,' she said at last.

And he wasn't about to give up. 'You'll be my honoured guest tonight.'

'Better that than dishonoured—and you can put *that* away,' she flashed when he pulled out his wallet.

'For the dress you'll be wearing tonight,' he explained.

She tightened her lips. Now he'd offended her. 'I'm not entirely penniless. I'm sure I can rustle something up.'

'Then, you agree?'

She looked at him and heaved a theatrical sigh. 'You got me,' she admitted.

'Just one thing. Don't keep me waiting when I pick you up tonight.'

'Making conditions now? I can always change my mind.'

'You won't,' he said confidently.

'And you can keep the killer smile for someone who will appreciate it,' she added with a mock-stern frown.

'Someone like you?' he suggested, staring deep into her eyes.

'I've changed my mind. I'd be right out of my depth—and crazy to agree.'

'Too late. The deal is done.'

'No, it isn't,' Lucy argued, 'and now you're making me late for work.'

'You're making yourself late for work by taking so long to confirm the details of our date tonight.'

'Please take your hand off the door and let me go in.'

'No sense of adventure?' he said, going nowhere. 'I thought a lot more of you than that.'

'I've got plenty of sense of adventure,' Lucy assured him, 'and plenty of common sense too.'

'Prove it,' he said.

'I will, by refusing an invitation from someone I hardly know.'

'Every relationship has to start somewhere...'

Tadj looked so sexy, leaning against the door. Say yes to this ridiculous proposal and she could at least satisfy her workmates' curiosity about the *Sapphire*, as well as her own about Tadj. Say no, and she might regret it for the rest of her life.

'I'm not sure about risking my virtue on board that ship tonight,' she said, voicing her thoughts out loud.

'Your virtue?' Tadj commented with amusement. 'I didn't know that was on offer.'

'It isn't,' she said with a steely look.

'Shame,' he murmured, but with humour tugging at his mouth.

'Okay,' she said, decision made. She trusted herself to act sensibly if she accepted his invitation, and it was the opportunity of a lifetime. 'I have decided to come to the party tonight.'

'Excellent.'

Tadj's wolfish smile sent tremors to all her erogenous zones, to the point where she almost missed him adding, 'No tiaras. It's just a casual get-together.'

'Between billionaires?' she suggested.

'Between you and me,' he corrected her.

All she had to do was laugh it off and walk through that door. She need never see him again. Life would return to normal. But normal could be boring, and Tadj was right about adventure beckoning, but only if the adventure was on her terms.

'Don't *you* be late,' she warned. 'It's cold at night, standing in this doorway.'

CHAPTER THREE

WHAT HAD SHE DONE? *What had she done?* How had she allowed herself to be talked into this? Wicked eyes blazing into hers hadn't helped, Lucy reflected later as she got ready in her small bedsit above the laundry. Nor had feeling as if Tadj and she had known each other longer than it took to drink a couple of cups of coffee. But now was not the time to reflect on why it was possible to feel like that about someone, and not about others. Her decision to go to the party had been made, and she had no intention of skulking in her room, or asking her friends to send Tadj away when he arrived. It would be fascinating to discover how the other half lived, and she could report back to her friends at the laundry.

The only remaining problem was what to wear. She had one decent dress; a cheap sale-rail spectacular she still wasn't entirely sure was her colour. Red hair and freckles didn't always blend well with bright red, especially when the weather turned her skin blue with cold. She'd only worn it once, to the Christmas party when everyone made an effort for the sake of the elderly owner of the laundry. Miss Francine went to so much trouble for them, it was the least they could do.

So... Tadj was older than she was, and obviously more

sophisticated, and much richer, suggesting he'd be used to women in designer clothes. Too bad, she thought as she plucked the dress from its hanger. He'd pressed her to accompany him tonight, so he'd have to put up with her dress being a bit too short and too tight. The sale rail didn't offer custom made.

Tadj must be around early thirties, she thought. She was twenty-three, and definitely not glamorous, or sophisticated. Or successful...not yet. But she could keep a roof over her head, which was something to be proud about, and she had the best of friends, which was more important than anything else. And she had no intention of putting out for the price of a gourmet meal, let alone a date on board the flashiest vessel in the harbour, Lucy determined, firming her jaw. A polite thank-you note would have to be enough, she concluded as a noisy group of excited friends, having spied on her from inside the laundry while she was negotiating with Tadj, burst into the room.

'So?' they chorused, nearly deafening her as they gathered around. 'You've been seen.'

'Really?' She acted daft.

'With the best-looking man on King's Dock,' one of them confided with a jerk of her head to her friends.

'Hmm.' Staring heavenwards, Lucy pretended to think about this. If she'd had more experience of men, maybe she could have joked along with her girlfriends, but somehow Tadj was special—unique in her experience—and she didn't want to exchange banter concerning him while the tender green shoot of a first meeting was still so fragile. 'I did meet someone who works in security,' she admitted frankly. 'He bought me coffee, and that's all there is to it.'

'So you won't be seeing him again?' her friends pressed, exchanging knowing glances with each other.

'I didn't say that. What?' she demanded when her girl-friends started to laugh.

'It's not what you're telling us, but what you're not telling us,' one of them insisted. 'Unless, of course, you really don't know?'

'Don't know what?' She'd been warm and safe here, and surrounded by friends since the day she'd arrived. Had she thrown all that away for the sake of a wicked smile and mocking eyes?

'Didn't the guy tell you his name?' one of her closest friends prompted.

'His name is Tadj. He doesn't have to hide anything,' Lucy insisted.

But did he? she wondered. The spear of anxiety had returned, and with it thoughts of her vicious gangland thug of a stepfather, who was currently serving a lengthy term in prison for his crimes. He had plenty to hide, and could still charm the pants off anyone who didn't know his reputation, and who met him for the first time.

'Tadj,' another friend prompted, breaking into Lucy's troubled thoughts. 'Did this Tadj have a surname?'

It was a relief when Tadj's stunningly attractive face swam into Lucy's mind, completely eclipsing the evil mask of her stepfather. 'I don't think so,' she murmured as she racked her brains. 'First names are enough at a first encounter over coffee.'

'Did he tell you about his job?' another friend pressed.

'Yes—security. I already told you.'

Her stepfather had eyes like a shark, black, dead and cold, she remembered, without a flicker of expression in them. There was no evil in Tadj's eyes. He could look a bit fierce at times—all right, most of the time—but there was also good humour and warmth. And, of course, the sexual heat that flared off him. Better not to think about that now.

More friends had joined them, and her tiny room was overcrowded. Miss Francine was known locally as the Old Woman Who Lived in a Shoe, because of her generosity towards the women she hired. The bedsits she let out for a peppercorn rent might be cramped and old-fashioned, but, for women seeking sanctuary, not even the finest five-star hotel could compare.

'So, I've been seen with a man,' Lucy accepted with a good-humoured shrug, making a joke of it as she stared around.

'With the Emir of Qalala, no less,' her best friend informed the rest.

Lucy froze like a child playing statues. 'What did you say?'

She had heard perfectly well, but…*the Emir of Qalala*? *Tadj was the Emir of Qalala*?

She tried and failed to process the information. And what was she supposed to say now? *I'm a dope—I didn't recognise him? I didn't read the papers today? I don't watch local TV?* All true, unfortunately.

'Oh, come on—potential Emira,' her friends coaxed. 'Tell us what the Emir is really like…'

'I'm afraid I don't know,' Lucy admitted. 'He seems nice enough.'

'And as hot as hell,' one of her friends put in to an agreeing chorus of raunchy suggestions.

'Might have been,' Lucy conceded.

'His photograph is all over the news,' another friend

insisted, in a tone that said she should have known. 'And nice doesn't begin to describe him.'

'Sex on two hard-muscled legs,' someone else shouted out.

'With a body made for sin,' another drooled as she thrust a magazine cover in front of Lucy's nose.

Lucy inhaled sharply at the sight of Tadj, tanned and buff, wearing a pair of figure-hugging swim shorts.

'Either he's a prize-winning swimmer, or he likes to show that thing off.'

'Stop,' Lucy implored her friends. 'I had a coffee with him, nothing more.'

'He'd definitely need security if I shared a hot drink with him,' a friend exclaimed as she read the article over Lucy's shoulder. 'And he's one of the infamous Sapphire Sheikhs—so-called because they are as rich as Croesus, and as insatiable as a pack of ravening wolves.'

Lucy's pulse raced off the scale. So Tadj was not only ridiculously wealthy, but all-powerful and royal too. It was too late to refuse his invitation without appearing to be a coward. She didn't have a number to call him, and she could hardly breach security to ask one of his men to deliver a message. Out of her depth and out of her mind didn't even begin to cover this mess! Adventure was one thing, but not on this scale.

'The Emir of Qalala,' she murmured, biting her lip, turning away as she tried to reconcile the little she knew about a hot guy in a café who had turned out to be one of the world-renowned Sapphire Sheikhs. 'I had no idea,' she murmured.

And if she had, would she have accepted Tadj's invitation?

He was an extraordinary man, and, yes, she probably

would have taken the chance. Did his title make a difference? He'd asked if money could change her opinion. She'd never considered a royal title, but she understood that great privilege came with restrictions and complications. Her usual good humour kicked in at this point. No half measures. If she was going to dip her toe in the dating pool, why not go for full-body immersion? She wouldn't simply be out of her depth at the Sheikh's party, she'd be like Orphan Annie at the feast, but that chance to peep inside a very different world proved irresistible. Spinning around, she faced her friends. 'Could you help me get ready for tonight?'

When they chorused, 'Yes!' she knew there was no turning back.

Security expert indeed, Lucy thought as her friends jostled around. Just wait until she saw Tadj again! 'I own one dress, and no high-heeled shoes,' she explained. 'My dress is sleeveless and it will be freezing out tonight. If I could also borrow an evening bag, big enough for a lip gloss and my bus fare home?'

Drowned out by laughter and offers of help, she made a silent promise that she would be safely tucked up in her own bed by midnight.

He'd never been uncertain of a woman. He should have brought Lucy back with him to make sure he'd see her again, Tadj concluded as he strode on board his friend's superyacht. Lucy was unique and unpredictable. There were no guarantees she'd show up tonight. For once, that really mattered to him.

'All women are unique, my friend,' his friend Sheikh Khalid insisted when they met on his arrival in the grand salon. 'You seem preoccupied,' the Sheikh added when Tadj grimaced.

'Unfinished business,' he supplied economically. Usually, he would welcome both Khalid's company and his interest, but not this time, because all he wanted to think about was Lucy.

Walking out on deck, he scanned the dock as if she might suddenly appear. Was her head buried in one of her college books, or was she getting ready for the party? There was no way to tell.

'What do you do with a woman you can't read?' he asked Khalid as his friend joined him out on deck.

'Bed her?'

'That's not helpful.'

'It's always a good start,' Khalid argued with an ironic smile.

Everything on board the *Sapphire* was geared towards seduction tonight, Tadj thought as they both pulled away from the rail. An army of talented florists was currently adding last-minute touches to the container-loads of exotic blooms.

'You'll be staying in the Golden Suite,' Khalid informed him, 'if that suits you. Make the most of it while you can.'

They shared a wry laugh. 'That temple to all things gold,' Tadj commented. 'It's enough to put anyone off their stride with the addition of those outrageous erotic hangings.'

'Not you, my friend,' Khalid assured him. 'I would have thought you found those hangings rather tame.'

'If I didn't know you better, I'd think you were trying to set me up with this woman,' Tadj responded.

'How could that be true?' Khalid queried. 'I've only

just learned about her. But, good hunting—you'd be surprised how many women are delighted to be seduced in the Golden Suite.'

'No doubt spurred on by the inspiration provided by the artwork,' Tadj commented dryly. 'But this one's different.'

'Different how? She's a woman, isn't she?'

Seeing his expression, Khalid shrugged. 'You've got it bad, my friend.'

Bad? Tadj ground his jaw as he sprang out of the *Sapphire*'s lap pool. Bad was putting it mildly. Grabbing a towel, he dried his exercise-pumped body with impatience. Warnings should be issued with Lucy, that she could change the direction of his thoughts within ten minutes of meeting her. Even exercise hadn't helped him today. He'd never known anything like this. Women didn't get to him; he got to them. Lucy was so young and unsophisticated, she couldn't know the tricks that others played. Funny, blunt and challenging, she was absolutely irresistible, and irresistible was the one thing he didn't need. His usual type knew the score, and were sophisticated enough to use him for what they wanted, without complication. The feeling was mutual, but he couldn't be that way with Lucy. Innocence came at a price, and, though he was no saint, the thought of waking her to physical pleasure was driving him crazy.

Having dressed and checked every timepiece and lump of tech on board in order to convince himself that minutes really could tick by so slowly, he parked the shave and transferred his pacing from ship to shore. He hadn't experienced this level of anticipation since he'd been an overeager youth. When he spotted Lucy standing in the doorway of the laundry, it was as if an atomic reaction went off in his brain. They locked eyes, and he walked towards her. It was the challenge on her face that aroused him. Her body language said she knew who he was, and intended to make him pay for withholding the information.

'You have a lot of explaining to do,' she said.

All he was aware of now was her intoxicating wild-flower scent.

'Am I late?' he said, glancing at his wristwatch and frowning, as if he didn't know what she meant.

'Don't try that on me,' she warned him, narrowing her astonishing jade-green eyes in the very best type of threat.

'Good evening to you too,' he murmured mildly, maintaining eye contact.

'Good evening, Your *Majesty*.'

'My name is Tadj,' he reminded her quietly.

'The Emir of Qalala, I believe.'

He wanted to kiss her as her expressive mouth twisted in a wry smile.

'What are you doing?' she protested as he dragged her close.

'What does a title change about me?'

'Everything,' she said as he brushed her lips teasingly with his. 'Are you going to let me go now?'

'No.'

The first kiss was extraordinary in that it fired every part of him, and made it vital there were more. 'Let's start over,' he said, releasing her before she was quite ready. 'Good evening,' he murmured.

'Good evening, Your Majesty,' she teased him, still trying to catch her breath. They stared at each other with a mixture of acceptance and humour. 'You've got a long way to go to recover your credibility,' she warned, testing her kiss-bruised lips with the tip of her tongue.

'More tolerance required,' he suggested.

'On my part?' she queried.

'Yes, on your part,' he confirmed. 'Shall we?' He glanced in the direction of the super yacht.

The *Sapphire* was a fabulous vessel. Even he was impressed from here, where he could appreciate every inch of it, blazing with light from bow to stern. Party planners had been working tirelessly all day to create a fairyland for the guests, and, though she might still be reeling from the unexpected start to their evening, even Lucy couldn't hide her excitement.

'No more deception, and no more surprises,' she warned as they approached the security gates. 'Promise—or I'm not going any further.'

'When you look at me like that…'

'What?' she murmured, her eyes darkening.

He would promise her almost anything, he thought, but sensibly confined himself to a wry smile and a shrug.

'So you're really the Emir of Qalala?' she said as the security guards waved them through.

'I really am,' he confirmed.

'I'm impressed.'

'No, you're not,' he argued with amusement. 'Not by my title, anyway.'

'Are you always so confident?'

'Always.' Except for tonight, he thought, because Lucy was a whole new experience.

'You're one of the infamous Sapphire Sheikhs,' she observed. 'That alone is supposed to impress me, isn't it?'

'Legendary, rather than infamous, I'd hope.'

She shrugged and halted. 'You should have told me you're one of the world's richest men.'

'Told you, why?' he asked. They were approaching the gangplank where a queue of guests was forming.

'Because it makes us very different,' she said.

'If we're so ill matched, why are you here? For a glimpse into the life of the super-rich?'

'That's part of it,' she admitted frankly.

If he'd been looking for a smooth-tongued casual date, a woman who would do and say everything she could to impress him, he'd got it badly wrong—and thank goodness for that!

CHAPTER FOUR

'Sir...'

One of the security guards, having recognised Tadj, escorted them to a second boarding point a bit further along than the first.

'What's that the other guests are holding?' Lucy asked him as she gazed at those queuing patiently to have their identities checked before being allowed on board.

This was her first taste of life on the other side of the Sapphire Sheikh divide, he reminded himself as he explained, 'Sheikh Khalid's invitations have been issued in silver boxes, studded with sapphires.'

'Recyclable, I hope,' she teased him with a cheeky smile.

'Yes,' he confirmed, matching her mood. 'The box has to be large enough to hold a passport and other documentation, such as a visa.'

'You need passports to get on board?' Lucy exclaimed, staring up at him with an engaging mix of indignation and surprise.

'Only when certain guests disembark in certain countries,' he explained with a shrug. 'The party doesn't last for one night,' he added when she looked at him in bemusement. 'It lasts at least a week.'

'Not for me, it doesn't,' she assured him. 'And, any-way, I don't have my passport with me.'

'None needed,' he confirmed. 'The umbrella of dip-lomatic immunity covers both of us.'

'I beg your pardon?' she said, turning serious and concerned. 'I haven't signed up for a cruise. A couple of hours with you will be enough.'

'For me too,' he assured her dryly.

They laughed so easily now, but then she flashed him a look to warn that her next statement must be taken se-riously. 'I have to be back by midnight,' she said, 'or alarms will ring at the laundry, and the police will come looking for me. I made sure everyone knows where I am tonight,' she explained.

'Nice to know you trust me,' he mocked lightly, 'but sensible.'

'I thought so,' she agreed. 'I don't take chances.'

'Nor should you,' he confirmed as a uniformed officer stepped forward to escort them on deck. He liked Lucy more and more, and couldn't help comparing her to all the other women who wound around him like clinging vines in the hope that things might progress. Not Lucy. She slapped her cards down on the table face up, no nonsense.

'So, Your Importance,' she murmured as they walked ahead of the other guests, 'privilege all the way for you. What am I supposed to call you in front of people?'

'Nothing rude.'

'Then, be nice to me.'

'I intend to be,' he assured her. 'Call me Tadj—or Lord and Master, if you prefer.'

'Tadj will do nicely,' she said.

'Sir...'

'Yes?' He glanced sideways at the officer detailed to escort them.

'Sheikh Khalid is waiting to greet you.'

He glanced up and saw his striking friend watching their embarkation with amusement. 'Of course,' he murmured, acknowledging the officer with a brief dip of his head. 'Come on,' he added to Lucy. 'There's a lot I want you to see before you meet our host.' He didn't feel like sharing her. 'I don't want you to miss a single moment on board the *Sapphire* tonight.'

His determination intensified as Lucy's eyes sparkled with excitement; whether that was for him, or for this fabulous event, for once, he didn't know.

This was partying on a scale Lucy could never have imagined, even in her wildest fantasy. Jewel-studded boxes to hold the invitations...guests in diamonds, exuding clouds of exclusive scent...limos lined up on the dock as more guests arrived, and then those guests being made to stand in line while Lucy walked past on the arm of the Emir of Qalala. That was just crazy. Accepting that a vessel as huge as the *Sapphire* was privately owned took another immense leap of faith. There were so many decks, so many bands playing, so many guests milling about, and floral installations beyond magnificent that gave Kew Gardens at the height of summer a run for its money. The scent of blossom was intoxicating, as was the tang of ozone, but, above everything else, it was the smell of money, of outrageous wealth, that really threatened to choke her.

'Feeling nauseous?' Tadj commented when she made a noise down deep in her throat. 'And we're not even moving yet.'

'Nor will we, I hope,' she said, recovering fast. 'At least, not while I'm on board. I'm just feeling a bit out of place,' she admitted, 'amongst all these diamonds and pin-thin figures dressed in designer clothes.'

'Nonsense,' Tadj insisted with a dismissive wave of his hand. 'You're the most beautiful woman here. And the most intelligent.'

'Did you give everyone an IQ test?' she queried, with the reminder not to take herself so seriously. 'Okay, so you know most of the women here,' she remarked with a grin, as Tadj looked at her in a certain way. 'I should have known.'

'Most of them aren't renowned for their academic qualifications,' he admitted, 'but they have other qualities.'

'Spare me,' she begged. 'I don't need a rundown of the sordid details.'

'Relax. Enjoy yourself,' he advised.

Why not? This was incredible. 'Thank you for inviting me,' she said. It was just unfortunate that her gaze slipped to his mouth as she added, 'I've never seen anything like this before.'

He laughed softly down deep in his chest. 'Feast your eyes,' he invited.

She would. This was the Emir of Qalala, and the Emir of Qalala had kissed her. She had no idea if he would ever do so again, but she would remember that kiss for the rest of her life. He was one hot guy, so why not enjoy this as Tadj suggested? It wasn't every day that fantasy turned into the best type of reality. She liked him more and more. He was courteous and fun to be with, and as hot as hell.

'Drink?' he suggested.

'Sparkling water, please.' Must keep a level head, she

warned herself, and something told her that wouldn't be easy tonight.

'Sparkling water, *mademoiselle*?' a steward invited, handing Lucy a crystal glass.

'Are you hungry?' Tadj enquired when the steward had left them.

'Shouldn't we go and meet our host?' she asked, wishing her body wouldn't respond quite so willingly to the amused heat in Tadj's eyes.

'No hurry. The other guests will keep him busy for a while.'

'I'm okay with water for now, thank you.' How could she eat while her senses were being subjected to an overload of testosterone? Tadj made her long for all things forbidden, and she had to remind herself that she was nothing more than a dockside novelty for him.

Several wine fountains had been installed on board the *Sapphire*, and it was here that couples seemed to be congregating. She couldn't stop staring at them—arms entwined, bodies touching, laughing intimately into each other's faces.

'Would you like me to fill your glass?' Tadj prompted with a curving smile as he glanced at the glittering stream.

For a moment she was lost for words, and then came to with a jolt. 'No, thank you. I'm steering clear of the hard stuff tonight, and only drinking water.'

He laughed. 'Sensible.'

'Always,' she confirmed.

They stared at each other for a few potent moments, during which time Tadj looked like a mythical hero, while she tried to stop her cheeks flaming red. But if there was a cure for blushing, she hadn't found it yet, something to do with her pale Celtic skin that showed every emotion whether she wanted it to or not.

'Why did you invite me tonight?'

'Fireworks,' he said.

She blinked and then realised what he meant as plumes of light began to explode all around the ship. 'I really want to know,' she pressed.

This was dangerous. She was always so cool where men were concerned, and with good reason, having the experience of her stepfather behind her, but with Tadj cool was becoming increasingly impossible.

'Look!'

His touch on her arm made her jump, and it took her a moment to follow his stare to the circus performers in glittering green costumes, swinging high over their heads. She gasped, and not just because of the risks the acrobats were taking, but because Tadj had swung an arm possessively around her shoulders, which was a risk right here.

'And down there,' he said as she was about to wriggle free.

And breathe, Lucy instructed herself firmly, making herself relax as Tadj turned her to see the fire-eaters and jugglers performing.

'We've got a lot more to see,' he said as he moved and took her with him across the deck.

He wasn't joking. The next place they stopped had been transformed into a souk, complete with flower stalls and food outlets, as well as flashy gifts of every type. The attendants behind the stalls were exotically and colourfully robed, and played a good part as they shouted their wares to the passing guests. No money changed hands, and there was quite a crowd competing for the hats, shawls, beads and ornaments, with which to adorn their designer clothes.

'This isn't a party, it's a theatrical production,' Lucy commented as she glanced up at Tadj.

'One man's ludicrous is another man's normal,' he remarked. 'And you look sensational, by the way,' he added as they walked on. 'No need for strings of beads, or even a hat to hide your face.'

'Watch it, mister,' she said, smiling as she faked a punch, and Tadj ducked. 'Actually, you don't look bad yourself, now I take a proper look…' Massive understatement. Tadj looked sensational in nothing more than a pair of well-cut jeans and an open-neck shirt, with a casual jacket left open to reveal his powerful chest. He could have worn a boiler suit, and still looked fabulous. Better still naked, she thought.

And here she was in borrowed clothes, carrying the flag for her friends. Tipping up her chin, she met his teasing stare head-on, and was rewarded by the warmth in Tadj's eyes. Make that heat, she thought as her body responded with enthusiasm.

'Champagne?' Tadj proposed as he selected two crystal flutes from a tray a passing waiter was carrying.

'No, thanks. I'm a cheap drunk, so I'll stick to water, if you don't mind. And even if you do,' she added good-humouredly. Tonight was going better than expected—far better than she'd dared to hope.

'To us,' he said as they raised their glasses.

'To a wonderful evening,' Lucy replied, calling on her natural caution. She might be having the time of her life—might have kissed the hottest man at the party, but she had no intention of completely losing her head.

Tadj achieved the impossible, by finding them a quiet

and sheltered spot on the *Sapphire*'s crowded deck. Taking her glass out of her hand, he put it down next to his. *Was he going to kiss her again?* Every part of her body tingled at the thought. She could feel him in every fibre of her being, as if he were the virtuoso who had temporarily laid aside his violin. Her strings were certainly twanging at the memory of his touch, Lucy thought, carefully concealing her amusement at a body running riot while the sensible head supposedly guiding it was temporarily unavailable.

'It's so beautiful here,' she said, looking around. The floral decorations were incredible, though the blossom was in a more restrained colour palette than the rest of the *Sapphire*, as if this area had been designed for lovers. It was like standing in the middle of a fragrant ocean of palest pink and white. Drawing on the heady scent, she closed her eyes, only for the unwelcome thought that she should be leaving soon to pop into her head. 'Tadj, I...'

'Tadj what?' he murmured.

He'd dipped his head to stare into her eyes, and their mouths were almost touching.

'Don't,' she begged.

'Why not?' he teased.

Her lips were tingling. His warm, clean, spicy scent was drugging her senses. She wanted another kiss and was in no hurry to move. Sighing raggedly as he began to tease her lips with his, she wondered if anything that felt this good could be bad for her. The touch of Tadj's hands on her arms was so light and yet so dangerous. She didn't want to break away. She wanted more of his skilful touches. He was so gentle, and yet so firm in a way she had never experienced before. He promised more pleasure than she could imagine.

'Something amusing you?' he asked, frowning as he stared down.

True, her mood had changed and no wonder. 'This *is* a film set,' she said, as a cloud of pink smoke drifted up from a lower deck, threatening to envelop them in its scented embrace.

'Where you are, anything's possible,' Tadj said dryly as he wafted it away. 'Look down there, and you'll see an oasis complete with sandy beach and palm trees.'

'And all for the amusement of the Sheikh's guests,' Lucy commented with a wry smile. 'And what about up here?' she queried softly, holding Tadj's burning stare.

He gave her a considering look. 'Up here you will find two people, namely you and me, who have more sense than to be taken in by a fantasy.'

If only, she thought as he smiled faintly. Tadj might have his sensible head screwed on tightly, but she'd lost hers when he'd kissed her.

'You're beautiful,' he whispered just as she was reflecting that there would never be another night like this.

'No, I'm not,' she said. 'I'm just okay, but you're beautiful.' When he frowned at this, she added, 'All right, then, you're not just beautiful, you're rugged and tough too.'

'That's better,' he agreed with a grin. 'But it's only your opinion.'

'And I'm always right,' she said.

He laughed and, cupping her chin in one hand, he kissed her again. By the time he'd finished kissing her, she was ready to agree to anything he suggested. Deep down, she knew she should move away, slow things down, but she couldn't—she didn't want to. She wanted more breath-stealing kisses, and more caresses from those knowing hands. More than ready to accept that one night couldn't last for ever, she knew that memories like these would stand the test of time.

The cloud of pink smoke added to the sense of unreality, making things seem possible that she would never have considered on a regular first date. Being close to Tadj and touching him like this was as far from Lucy's normal as it was possible to get. This was definitely the most romantic night of her life, she thought as she stared into his dark, compelling stare, and she was in no hurry to put the brakes on.

Everything about Lucy enchanted him. She felt perfect beneath his hands, and was full of surprises. Passion of all types fired off her, and she wasn't afraid to stand up to him. Quirky and inexperienced, as he had thought her, she had responded to his kisses, not on his terms, but on hers, and he liked that about Lucy best of all. He admired her openness. What you saw was what you got, and the night was just beginning.

'Nice dress,' he remarked as she straightened the folds of fabric, smoothing it over her thighs, as he would like to do.

'I have my friends to thank for helping me put this outfit together,' she admitted. 'Oh, I see,' she said, reading him with her usual ease. 'You like the dress because it leaves my back bare.'

'That's part of it,' he admitted. The tasteful knee-length dress was Lucy's choice, he guessed. The glittering shoulder bag encrusted with diamanté, together with its matching high-heeled shoes, didn't strike him as Lucy's taste. She was all about understatement, and the shoes were too big, which kind of gave it away. The sensible, if dated poncho she'd handed over to an attendant at the entrance to the *Sapphire* would certainly keep her warm, but he couldn't imagine Lucy spending her hard-earned cash on such a bulky and unflattering item. 'You've got some good friends,' he commented.

'The best,' she agreed.

The fact so many people had wanted to contribute to Lucy enjoying herself tonight told him a lot about her character, as well as her resourcefulness, not to mention good judgement when it came to choosing her friends.

'Let's make a move,' he suggested as a fresh wave of pink mist made its way towards them from the lower deck. Taking hold of her hand, he linked their fingers as he led her towards the infamous Golden Suite on board the *Sapphire*.

'Shouldn't we meet the Sheikh first?' she asked, glancing over her shoulder as impatience to have her truly alone led him to increase his pace.

'He's not going anywhere.'

But they were, Lucy thought. And where was Tadj taking her? Her sensible mind caused her to worry her bottom lip, but her wayward body thrilled as she considered the possibilities.

CHAPTER FIVE

TADJ HAD EXPLAINED that the stateroom he was about to show Lucy was unique. Not only was it full of treasures beyond compare in the historical sense, but also it was stuffed to the gunnels with golden ornaments and furniture, as well as the fabulous, famous sapphires.

'Do I get to see your etchings too?' she asked lightly.

'No etchings. Erotic hangings,' Tadj informed her. 'No joke,' he assured Lucy when she looked at him in surprise. 'So, I hope you're not easily shocked.'

'Me? No,' she said on a throat turned suddenly dry.

'Extremely erotic hangings,' Tadj teased, seeing her discomfort.

'I'm not entirely unaware of the workings of the human body.'

He laughed. 'These aren't so much workings, as the most outlandish contortions.'

Lucy gave him one of her 'so you think I'm dumb' looks. 'Well, it sounds like a very special room.'

'Sarcastic,' he commented, smiling faintly.

'Curious,' she said honestly. And then she frowned. 'But it doesn't sound much like a room for lingering in.'

'You might change your mind.'

'I doubt it.'

This was a deck reserved for *very* special guests, Lucy thought as a security guard, having recognised Tadj, stood back to let them through. The corridor was as luxurious as everywhere else on the ship, with plush carpets, pristine ivory walls, decorated with fascinating *objets d'art*, all shown to best advantage by discreet lighting. Plump upholstered seating invited a pause at convenient intervals—goodness knew what went on there, Lucy thought, but Tadj wasn't interested in lagging behind to explain, and curiosity propelled her forward. For some crazy reason, she trusted him. With no real foundation, that was reckless maybe, but she had a good feeling about him that she couldn't explain.

Even so, it was better not to take any chances, she thought as he stopped outside the most stunning golden door. 'Five minutes and I'm out of here,' she warned in a teasing tone to soften the information.

Seemingly unconcerned, he shrugged.

'I'm impressed,' Lucy admitted as she stood back to admire the door's intricate ornamentation.

'Wait until you see inside,' Tadj advised. Opening the door, he invited her to enter the Golden Chamber.

Having overdosed on luxury for the past hour or so, Lucy was complacent, thinking she was ready for anything, but her first sight of the unique room stunned her into silence. It was so bling, she wasn't sure if she liked it or not. But, 'Wow,' she exclaimed as she stared around. Her feet sank into a carpet that was deep, sapphire-blue, while every surface, wall, ceiling, and piece of furniture was composed of solid gold. She guessed the ornaments would be the same, and these were studded with glowing blue sapphires, and were quite obviously precious artefacts from some ancient time.

'I'm not sure about the elevator music,' she teased Tadj, turning to face him and raise a brow at the strings playing softly in the background.

He laughed. 'Me neither. I guess it's supposed to improve the ambience.'

'It smells good, anyway,' Lucy conceded. Incense was burning in golden salvers, and, closing her eyes, she drew deep on the exotic scent.

'Time to look at the shocking hangings,' she said matter-of-factly, opening her eyes. She stared around, but her gaze always returned to Tadj. He was more interesting than the erotic hangings, though she did have a few questions for him.

'Is that pose even possible?' she asked, tipping her head to one side. 'I had no idea human bodies were even capable of doing that.' She wasn't easily shocked, just perplexed.

Smiling his unreadable smile, Tadj made no answer. Opening a second, heavily ornamented door, he revealed another glittering golden stateroom, one so large it easily accommodated several glittering crystal chandeliers.

To swing from? Lucy wondered.

'You're laughing,' Tadj commented with interest. 'Don't you like it?'

'Sensory overload,' Lucy explained. 'Otherwise, I actually feel quite humble to be invited here to see what must be one of the hidden wonders of the world.'

'I'm glad you think so,' he said with a touch of humour in his tone.

She wasn't only thinking about that, but fantasising about Tadj lowering her slowly down on top of the thick, soft wool rug they were currently standing on.

'This is my topic,' she reminded him. 'The display

of important historical works of art falls well within my field of interest.'

'Then, I'm glad I brought you here,' he said.

Propping a hip against a console table that appeared to be made of solid gold, Tadj folded his arms and stared at her. 'You're hard to read,' he said. 'Tell me more about yourself...'

'Am I?' she said, ignoring the question. The connection between them was stronger than ever, and more than ever she wanted to stay and chat, but the atmosphere inside this room was just too seductive. 'I can't stay too long at the party,' she said in a reminder to them both, 'and I want to make the most of it,' she added, moving towards the door. 'I have responsibilities.'

'As do I,' Tadj assured her.

Stalemate. Several tense seconds ticked by, while Lucy gazed out at the brilliantly lit marina, where the bustle of ordinary life carried on in what seemed like a million miles from where they were standing. She'd be back there soon enough. She certainly wouldn't remain on board when *Sapphire* slipped its moorings.

'Penny for them?' Tadj prompted.

Turning, she lifted her chin so she could stare him in the eyes. 'I'm just taking everything in—you...me...this,' she admitted, glancing around. 'Very soon the *Sapphire* will sail, and you'll sail with it.'

'Will you miss me?' he teased.

'No,' she lied. The time had come to examine her feelings, and decide whether to stay, or go.

He sensed the change in Lucy. From pure enjoyment and wonder, she had paused to consider her feelings, and where she fitted into this scenario. Her decision was typical Lucy, in that it both pleased and surprised him.

'I want you,' she whispered with a shrug of her slender shoulders.

Her candour fired his hunger as nothing else could. Slowly drawing her towards him, he kissed her neck, before brushing her lips teasingly with his. Turning in his arms, she rested back against his chest, so he kissed her again and felt her tremble. Innocence demanded a measured response, and for once in his life he wasn't sure he was in full command of his control.

'Isn't this beautiful?' she murmured, staring out of the floor-to-ceiling balcony window, to where the soft pop of gunpowder heralded the sight of fireworks bursting into vivid flame.

His answer was to rasp his stubble very lightly across her neck. The rush of light across the night sky seemed appropriate, somehow. Was there more to this than sex? Lucy was exceptional. And impatient, he concluded with amusement, as she moved restlessly in his arms. But she wasn't done surprising him just yet. Turning to face him, she reached up and laced her fingers through his hair, bringing him down to kiss her, as a far more experienced woman might have done. Instantly hard when she rubbed her lush, warm body against his, he mapped her breasts appreciatively and was rewarded by her nipples turning pebble-hard against his palm.

'Don't tease me,' she begged. 'By the way,' she added with one of her comic looks that only revealed how vulnerable she was feeling, 'you don't think I'm fat, do you?'

He smiled to reassure her, with what must surely be a perplexed expression on his face. 'Fat? You're perfect.'

She relaxed and smiled mischievously up at him. 'Then…?'

'Delay is the servant of pleasure.'

'Don't give me that,' she warned him teasingly. 'Give me you...'

'Your wish is my command.' Swinging her into his arms, he carried her into the bedroom. As he laid her down on crisply dressed sheets, it felt more like taking a lover of long standing to bed than a woman he'd just met. He had no explanation for this, other than to say being with Lucy felt right. Her freshness and inexperience had won him over, and introducing her to pleasure was the only thing on his mind.

'Tadj...'

As she reached for him, he stared into eyes that had turned black, apart from a small rim of jade green around her pupils. 'Soon,' he promised, and, dipping down so he could kiss her, he smiled against her softly yielding mouth.

'Now,' she argued hotly, digging her fingers into him.

Lifting his head, he stared down with amusement. 'You'll regret it, if you rush.'

'I'm prepared to risk it.' Then her mind switched up a gear. 'I'm tired of being steady and prudent,' she admitted. 'I want tonight to be different. You're different. And I trust you—sort of,' she added with a rueful smile.

'That's quite a responsibility you've given me,' he said, grinning down.

Running her small hands appreciatively over his shoulders, she commented, 'I think you can take it.'

Shrugging off his jacket, he dropped it on a chair. Lucy was already pulling at her dress. He helped her. In just a bra and thong, she was the Venus de Milo made flesh, unbelievably beautiful and lush—and wild with impatience. Yanking at the buttons on his shirt, she managed to pull a couple off. As they flew across the floor, he freed his sapphire cufflinks and put them safely out of reach. They didn't lose eye contact for a second while all this was going on, and by the time he'd kicked off his shoes, she was working on his belt. Snapping it out of its loops, she gave a sound of triumph and fell back.

'Hussy,' he accused as she greedily sucked in air.

'You bet,' she said. 'You don't know how long I've waited for this.'

'From the first moment you saw me in the café?'

She laughed. 'Something like that.'

'Still, savour the moment—make it last...'

'Not a chance,' she assured him.

He sucked in air between his teeth as she boldly brushed her hand over his body. Her hand was tiny and he was big. Lucy wasn't the only one being seduced here.

'You're loving this,' she gasped, her pupils huge and black with excitement. 'The chase, I mean. Have I spoiled it for you, by becoming the aggressor?'

'Not at all—and that might change soon,' he warned.

She shrugged, but for a moment he thought she seemed uncertain. He loved sex, and did nothing to stop her as she explored him with exquisite skill. Sex had never been so much fun before, he thought as she slipped her hand into his boxers. It was just a hunger like anything else, to be satisfied on demand. With Lucy, sex had become an open-ended possibility. Her lack of experience was no deterrent to enthusiasm. When she stared into his eyes, there was fire in the depth of the black, as if she was claiming her mate.

'Do you trust me?' she demanded.

In the moment it took to answer, he hooked a thumb into the neck of his shirt, ready to pull it over his head.

'Trust works both ways,' she insisted, stilling as she stared at him, waiting for his answer.

'Trust has to be earned,' he countered as he tossed his shirt aside.

The most plausible liars could arrive in the most pleasing of packages, he had discovered in his youth. Lucy had gone some way to wipe out his recollection of an older woman who had found it all too easy to convince a gullible young prince, whose brain had been firmly lodged below his belt at the time, that fate intended them to be together. To help fate along, a loan from Tadj would really help her to build her business, she'd said. The jewels she'd plundered from the Emir's palace were to form part of an important exhibition, she had explained in court, after walking out on him in the middle of the night. His heart had turned to stone when her duplicity had been uncovered, and he had focused his mind solely on Qalala, vowing never to be duped again. So yes, trust was an issue for him. It was as vital as the air he breathed, and he was always waiting to be disappointed. But he'd put all that aside for this one night.

'When you surrender to pleasure there are no barriers left,' he told Lucy as she undressed him.

'And none required,' she promised as her nimble fingers flew over his remaining clothes.

Placing her hands palms flat against Tadj's chest, Lucy indicated that she would set the pace. He could have thrown her back and done anything he wanted, but that was what she meant by trust. One night to remember for all the right reasons, she thought, though her inner self warned that one night wouldn't be nearly enough. It would have to be, she thought.

Beneath Tadj's control, she sensed a fire raging. She

had never felt like this…so excited and lustful, which was hardly surprising when he stood before her naked and magnificent, like a bronze cast by Michelangelo. Fear of sex with such a big man had quickly been replaced by a hunger to know him inside her. Tadj would put her needs first, of that she was sure. He was such a compelling presence, he had pushed all the horrors she'd witnessed at home behind her with no effort at all. If he hadn't been the Emir of Qalala, and she no one in particular, she could easily have fallen in love with him.

'My turn now,' he said.

There'd be no argument there, she thought as he deftly removed her bra, maintaining eye contact while he did so.

'Good?' he murmured, surely knowing that everything he did was so much better than good.

Lucy couldn't help her shiver of delight. Burying her face in Tadj's hard, warm chest, she listened to the steady beat of his heart. It calmed her, and seemed to promise that whatever happened next, she would know pleasure as never before. Stretching out his length alongside her, he proved to be even bigger than she'd imagined. Against him, she was like a slender twig with breasts— breasts he seemed to admire—and she gasped with pleasure when he gave them his attention. She craved him, ached for him, and only one thing could ease that, but Tadj appeared to be in no hurry to relieve her frustration. Moving down the bed, he began by massaging her feet and kissing them. Sensation overload, she thought as the pleasure transferred to her core. Turning her, he dropped kisses on the back of her knees. More sensation…more gasping for sufficient breath—she'd had no idea she was so sensitive.

She was naked apart from her tiny lace thong, and

shivering with arousal in his arms. Writhing against the sheets, she craved firmer contact and yearned for release. Tadj answered this with firm-handed strokes down the length of her back, as if he were taming a spirited pony. Shaking uncontrollably, she finally settled again, and had to wait to see what he'd do next.

'You're very sensitive,' he commented, as if this pleased him.

She could do no more than hum contentedly, though she cried out with excitement when Tadj transferred his skill to her thighs. Almost without knowing she was doing so, she parted her legs in a blatant invitation for him to explore. She had never ached with need like this before, and was almost begging by the time he allowed his fingertips to brush against her. Grabbing a pillow, she clutched it to her chest as if that could imbue her with the strength to wait.

'Turn onto your back,' he instructed.

His tone aroused her beyond bearing, and she hurried to do as he said.

Scraping his stubble across the very sensitive skin at the nape of her neck, he made her cry out with need. If this was being instructed in the art of pleasure, she was the most willing student there could ever be.

Resting her legs over his shoulders, Tadj concentrated his attention on that area that had waited so patiently, while she moaned softly and rhythmically as he attended to her needs with his tongue.

'Now,' he prompted in a low, yet commanding tone, and, lifting his head, he watched her reaction as he replaced the touch of his tongue with his hand.

She couldn't hold on—impossible. The thought that she was exposing herself, body and soul, flashed briefly across her mind, but carnal hunger had soon extinguished the last of her doubts, and she fell greedily, screaming repeatedly with pleasure as the most powerful release took her over.

'Good,' Tadj praised, soothing her with kisses as he slowly brought her down.

Good didn't even begin to describe what she had experienced. Clinging to him, she silently begged for more... and not so silently, which made him laugh, just a low chuckle down deep in his chest, but it was the feeling of closeness she valued most of all. She couldn't allow herself to believe that this must end. Tadj was so right for her in every way. There was only one thing wrong with that thought, which was that reality had to intrude at some point.

'Beautiful,' he whispered, pulling back.

She wasn't beautiful, but he made her feel beautiful. Somehow, her hang-ups deserted her with Tadj. Which was strange when the contrast between them was so stark. He was beautiful. Built like a gladiator, swarthy and tanned, he was tough, yet careful with her, and exceptionally easy on the eye. No other man could compare, which almost certainly meant she'd never have another lover. Fate was a cruel mistress. Tadj was the Emir of Qalala and out of reach, but that couldn't stop them enjoying each other's bodies.

'What's amusing you now?' he asked with one of his dark smiles.

'Just one of my fantasies,' she admitted.

'Forget fantasies,' he advised, moving over her. 'Reality is much more fun. And don't tense up when there's no need.'

Was he joking? It would take both her hands to encompass him, and then only just.

'I won't hurt you,' he promised. 'Greedy must wait,' he warned, teasing her with kisses as she thrashed her head about on the pillows.

'But not for long,' she argued fiercely.

Finding her needy place, he gave it his close attention, which brought her to the edge in moments. But just as she was about to tip over into pleasure, he withdrew his coaxing hand, leaving her panting and unsatisfied.

'Part your legs wider,' he commanded softly. 'That's better,' he approved. 'Now...' Reaching for a pillow, he slipped it beneath her buttocks, raising her even higher for his attention. She was completely exposed, completely vulnerable, which allowed Tadj to stimulate the area all around her sensitive core, without allowing her the release she so badly needed.

'I can't hold on,' she heard herself wail.

'You must,' Tadj insisted, 'or I'll stop.'

With a noisy gust of frustration, she raged, 'But I can't—I need it now!'

'You need *me* to teach *you* the benefit of restraint,' he argued softly.

'Just a bit more,' she begged in what she hoped was her most appealing voice.

'And have you lose control?' Tadj asked. He gave her one of his looks.

'Why shouldn't I lose control? Isn't that what this is about?'

'As I said, you have a lot to learn,' he told her. 'You will lose control, not once, but many times, if you listen to my instruction. Hold your legs open for me,' he commanded.

He only had to brush his fingertips across that painfully sensitive place to send her screaming off the edge. Arcing her body towards him, she thrust mindlessly in a rhythmical pattern that was an age-old hunt for union with her mate.

Tadj coolly denied her his hand. 'Wider,' he insisted.

By this point she was glad to do anything he suggested. 'More,' she managed on a shaking breath.

He brought her to the edge again, easing into her fractionally. When he withdrew, the agony of frustration was indescribable. Reaching out, she clamped her hands around his buttocks.

'Not yet,' he warned.

'I'm done with waiting,' she said fiercely, and as she spoke she claimed him. Tadj could have held her off with ease, but a line had been crossed, and they both knew it, and with a growl of triumph he pressed her into the bed, and took over.

However much he wanted this, wanted Lucy, he was determined to go slowly, so she would remember this for all the right reasons. However eager she might be, he would hold back. His body cried out for immediate satisfaction, but he ruled it ruthlessly. Pinning Lucy's hands above her head on the soft bank of pillows, he took her slowly and deeply, taking his time to make sure she savoured every moment of pleasure. His reward was that she lost control immediately, and as she bucked wildly beneath him he held her in position to ensure she explored what was possible.

Making love to Lucy was as natural as breathing. They each responded without the need for words, and grew closer, in amusement, in pleasure, in trust, in ways he'd never imagined possible with a woman, after knowing each other for so short a time. When she finally fell back exhausted, he smiled to think that the erotic hangings above the bed were tame by comparison with this.

'Do you never tire?' she asked when he stroked her into awareness again. Smiling into the pillows, she gave him an engaging sideways look. Curled up on the sheets like a contented pussycat, she made his stone heart long for the impossible, and so he took her again, turning his thoughts from complications to pleasure.

A long time later, he realised he was murmuring words in his own tongue to Lucy, and these were words he had never said to anyone. Whatever difficulties faced them, she was part of his life now. He had claimed her as she had claimed him, and, settling back with her safely nestled in his arms, he closed his eyes and they slept.

Dawn light woke Lucy when it streamed into the Golden Suite. Tadj lay sprawled across the bed. She had slept contentedly through the night in his embrace. He was so beautiful, she thought, staring down.

Hearing noises on deck, she was instantly alert. The consequence of being on board when the *Sapphire* left dock struck home forcefully, and, slipping out of bed without waking him, she went to peer out of the window. Her heart lurched as her worst fears were confirmed. The *Sapphire* was about to sail. Racing to drag on her clothes, she only knew that she had to get off before that happened, and there wasn't a moment to lose. Last night had been a wonderful dream, but she had always known she would wake up at some point. They both had their lives to live, and she didn't belong in this very different world. Tiptoeing back to the bed, she stared down wistfully, but some things could never be. Putting the past behind her had meant striving to move forward every day, and how could she do that if she stayed here? Wrenching her gaze away from the only man she could ever love, she left her heart with him, and hurried out of the room.

Tadj would move on when he tired of her, Lucy's sensible self insisted as she bolted down the gangplank. Life would continue as normal for the Emir of Qalala when the *Sapphire* sailed, while Lucy didn't have the luxury of taking time out.

Turning in response to the shouts of the sailors tossing ropes from shore to ship, she knew their strident voices were the death knell to the dreams she had so foolishly tucked away in her heart.

CHAPTER SIX

Three months later...

FROZEN TO THE spot on the tiled floor of the restaurant where she was working her second job on King's Dock, Lucy was stunned to see Tadj again. *How many more shocks could she take?*

As many as necessary, she told herself firmly after taking a few steadying breaths. Only an hour or so ago she had received a panicked phone call from her mother, to warn Lucy that her stepfather had unexpectedly received parole, and was due to be set free from prison, which meant they were both in danger. She had felt sick inside knowing there was an unborn child involved now.

And now this...

'Get away from here,' her mother had pleaded. 'It's the only way you can help me. You have to get out of the country, because if your stepfather finds you, he'll find a way to hurt me through you. Our lives are in danger, Lucy. I can't rest until I know you're safely out of his reach.' This was no exaggeration. Lucy knew only too well from past experience how dangerous her stepfather could be, and how utterly ruthless.

Holding Tadj's gaze steadily, she stamped on the urge

to tell him everything right away. She knew her eyes might give her away. Tadj had always been able to read her, and the fact that she was carrying his child couldn't be hidden for long. She didn't want to hide it—she was happy to think that in a few months' time there would be a baby—but she wasn't so certain how she felt about the fact that a child would bind them together for life, whether either of them wanted that or not.

'We meet again,' the Emir of Qalala intoned without a flicker of emotion on his dazzlingly handsome face.

She knew immediately that this was not the fun-loving guy from the café, but a very different animal, as Tadj regarded her as coolly as if they'd shared nothing more than a passing acquaintance. He'd drawn to a halt just a few steps away, and she could see nothing of the man she'd known in his eyes, yet somehow she must persuade this hostile stranger to take her away from here. This wasn't just a shock encounter, but a lucky quirk of fate that she must take advantage of. She'd go to Qalala, if she had to—whatever it took to keep her mother and baby safe.

All these thoughts were jangling in Lucy's head as they confronted each other. She would have liked more time to frame her argument and persuade him to take her with him, but there was no time.

With an almost imperceptible nod of his head, the Emir of Qalala summoned the maître d'. 'Lucy and I haven't seen each other for some time,' Tadj explained, 'and would appreciate your giving her the night off.'

This wasn't a question, but an instruction, Lucy thought as the maître d' gushed a response. Of course she could leave. 'Whatever suits you, Your Majesty,' he insisted.

The lift of one ebony brow was all it took for Tadj to

remind the maître d' that the Emir of Qalala was eating in his restaurant incognito, and that he didn't welcome reference to his royal status. This sent the hapless maître d' into a tailspin. 'I'll get your coat,' he told Lucy, rushing off.

At least fate was on her mother's side, Lucy thought as Tadj continued to stare at her. She'd had a genuine reason for leaving him three months ago, and could only hope that he didn't harbour grudges for long.

The distinguished gentleman who had been sitting with Tadj at the table made no complaint when his dining experience was brought to an abrupt end. Bowing politely over Lucy's hand, he excused himself, and within moments she noticed an official limousine sweeping away. So far, so good, she thought, as Tadj indicated that she should now sit down. 'We won't be staying long,' he told her. 'A glass of water, perhaps?'

If it hadn't been for her condition, a stiff brandy might have been more appropriate, Lucy reasoned, trying to dredge up some humour from what was a not so funny situation. Tadj's mention of leaving the restaurant was an additional reminder to keep a clear head. 'A glass of water would be nice,' she agreed, swallowing down her apprehension on a dry throat.

'Are you sure you're all right?' Tadj frowned. Cold as he was towards her, he was fundamentally a decent man. 'The shock of seeing me again hasn't been too much for you?'

The irony in his tone was the only warning she needed to be cautious, and she shot him a sharp look. Tadj's expression remained stony, while she remained silent. They had so much to say to each other, but the door of communication between them had slammed shut, and the mouth that had kissed her into oblivion remained set in a harsh line. Obviously, he was angry that she'd walked out on him. Who would do that to the Emir of Qalala? Who did that to anyone without a word of explanation? Lucy reflected unhappily, knowing she had to find a way to make this right, or the opportunity fate had so unexpectedly provided, to escape the country, and tell Tadj about their baby, would be lost.

She downed the water gratefully, and then plunged right in. 'I'm sorry I didn't say goodbye that night on the *Sapphire*, but you were asleep.'

'And you didn't think to wake me?'

He wasn't going to make this easy for her, and more than anything she wanted to tell him about the baby, but not here in a busy restaurant. It was such momentous news, she wanted to tell him in private so they could both take in what it meant.

'Perhaps you need something stronger than water?' Tadj suggested, in a way that warned he could read her easily.

Determined that she would not be bounced into blurting out the facts, she stated firmly, 'I never drink on duty, and I still have work to do.'

'You won't be working again tonight, so I don't see that's an issue.' His black stare dared her to disagree as he added, 'In my opinion a drink might settle you.'

'I hardly drink at the best of times,' she pointed out.

'And this isn't the best of times?'

Irony dripped off his every word. Sitting up straight, she came to a decision. No one could accuse her of being a coward. She had stood on her own two feet for long enough; she was about to become a mother. Not only had her stepfather failed to crush her spirit, she refused to run scared, and would do whatever it took to protect both her child and her mother, and when it came to defending herself she would fight. Drawing a deep breath, she said, 'I've got something to tell you.'

'You're pregnant,' Tadj stated without emotion.

Shock sucked the breath from her lungs. He'd guessed before she'd had chance to say anything. 'How did you know?'

'I know you,' he said. 'Three months?'

'Yes.'

'So my child,' he confirmed.

'Well, no other,' she said hotly.

The realisation that Lucy was expecting his child had hit him like a punch in the gut. He was about to become a father. What did he know about that? Precisely nothing. If he followed the example set by his socialite, uncaring father, the future of his child was grim.

Memories flooded back as he remembered how it felt to be the only child left sitting on his suitcase when the school holidays came around. Staff at the boarding school he'd attended had always done their best to make up for the neglect of his parents by calling Abdullah, a man who had cared for Tadj since Tadj was one of many in the nursery, to collect him from school. Being welcomed into Abdullah's happy family home had proved how children could live, not in palaces, but surrounded by love. How he'd longed for Abdullah to be his father, rather than to have been born a royal prince to parents who couldn't care less about him. Horror filled him at the thought that he could ever do that to a child. Stifling the dread, he moved on to practicalities that called for decisions, rather than maudlin recollections. He could have everything he wanted, including a ready-made family and a woman who had engaged his attention from the start, but this child would bind them together for life, which he hadn't planned for.

Lucy's face was pale and creased with worry as she waited for his reaction. His world had been jolted, but his logical mind had quickly kicked in. Safeguards must be put in place immediately for both mother and child. Three months ago, sex had been the only thing on his mind. He and Lucy had been lost in an erotic jungle, but they were back with far more than they'd set out with. He had no trouble accepting that he was the father of Lucy's child. No birth control was one hundred per cent effective. And on a positive note, the position of mistress was filled. He hadn't reckoned on a pregnant mistress, but putting Lucy and the child under his protection was vital, so the sooner he could get her away from here, the better.

Decision made, he stood. 'We're leaving,' he said, waiting for her to join him.

'Leaving?' Lucy flashed a glance outside, where another sleek black limousine had drawn up at the kerb.

'For my country house, and then on to Qalala,' he explained. 'We need to talk, and I'm not prepared to do that here.'

'Your country house?' Lucy queried, her voice shaking as if she was not quite in command of it. 'And then Qalala?'

Was he mistaken, or had she brightened at the prospect of leaving the country? No...she wasn't just pleased, she was relieved, he thought, as suspicion twisted inside him. 'We travel to my country house first, so that plans can be made for your arrival in Qalala. My staff need prior warning.'

Don't rock the boat, Lucy thought, though Tadj's tone

was chilling, and hardly boded well if she went with him now, but however cold he felt towards her for leaving him three months ago, and however shocked he might be about the baby, leaving the country was a priority, to keep her mother and her baby out of danger. What could be safer than leaving under the protection of the Emir of Qalala? Diplomatic protection would provide a safeguard from her vicious stepfather, leaving no loopholes for him to snake through.

Decision made, she stood, but then saw black-clad figures stepping out of the shadows. For a moment she thought her stepfather's thugs had found her, but when Tadj sent them off with a nod she realised they were his men. Out of the frying pan into the fire? she wondered.

'You don't need guards to make me come with you,' she told Tadj. 'I'll come quietly,' she added in a lame attempt at the humour they'd once shared.

Tadj said nothing, and seemed, if anything, more remote than ever. She had to give him a chance to get over the shock of learning she was expecting his baby, Lucy reminded herself. She wasn't the only one who'd been sent reeling with shock this evening.

'Now,' he prompted in a quiet, firm tone, glancing at the door.

She wasted a few more seconds, searching in vain for some sign of the warmth they'd once shared. Leaving the safe and familiar with a man she thought she knew, but suddenly couldn't be sure of, was quite an intimidating prospect. It was one thing knowing that Tadj was the Emir of Qalala, and quite another to feel the brush of his power.

'Get in,' he snapped when his chauffeur opened the door of the official limousine.

He joined her in the luxurious interior, but sat with his face averted as if he couldn't bear to look at her. Or, maybe he was deep in thought, Lucy reasoned. 'Are you kidnapping me?' she asked in an attempt to lighten the atmosphere.

'Are you over-dramatising?' he asked coldly as his driver closed the door.

No amount of luxury could soothe her in this confined space with a man who seemed so hostile. It takes two to tango, she wanted to tell him, but, so soon after her mother's alarming phone call, Lucy couldn't afford to rock the boat. This was the perfect opportunity to leave the country, and she couldn't allow anything to get in the way. His manner suggested that trust was a huge issue for Tadj, and if he suspected she was using him to escape her stepfather and keep her mother safe, she doubted he would ever forgive her.

'What have you been doing these past three months?' he demanded.

Jolted rudely back to the present, she turned to face him, and held his harsh stare steadily. 'I've been working…studying.' The moment she'd found out she was pregnant, she'd secured a second job at the restaurant close by the laundry, and was working hard to complete her studies at college. Her schedule didn't leave much spare time, but she'd needed the extra money for the deposit on a small garden flat she'd found close to King's Dock. With a tiny garden, this was where she had hoped to raise her child, but now her stepfather was free, she had to change her plans.

Everything had happened in such a rush, with Tadj appearing out of the blue and Lucy leaving with him. She would have to contact her employers, and talk to them both to explain that she was going away for a while. Luckily, college had broken up for the holidays, so that was one problem out of the way.

'Why, Lucy?'

'Why what?' Tadj's voice had shocked her tense and upright.

'Why did you walk out on me? Why have you taken so long to tell me about the baby? I thought we trusted each other.'

'We did—we do,' Lucy insisted.

Tadj's tone was harsh, and his black stare chilled her. She had the sense of clinging by her fingertips to any chance of having him take her out of the country where her stepfather couldn't find her, and use Lucy to blackmail her mother into allowing him back home.

Tadj's mouth twisted with scorn. 'Really?'

As he speared a disbelieving stare into her eyes, she hated the changes between them, and wished she could do something to bring back the man she'd met three months ago. He was so hostile she felt increasingly uncomfortable.

'You said we were going to your country house before we leave for Qalala. Is it much further?' She stared out of the window as the limousine sped along, only now realising how distracted she'd been, and how far they must have travelled.

'Does it matter?'

'Yes, of course it matters. People will miss me. They might call the police. I can't just disappear.'

Tadj's expression had blackened into a frown, making him appear even more intimidating. And alarmingly sexy, Lucy reluctantly conceded. The same attraction she'd felt three months ago still flashed between them like an unseen force.

'Why don't you call them, and reassure them?' he said.

'I would if I knew where we were going.'

Tone it down, Lucy thought. Arguing with the Emir of Qalala would get her nowhere. This wasn't the reasonable guy she'd met in a café, but someone else altogether.

And who was she?

A mother, Lucy thought as she folded her hands protectively over her still-flat stomach. She might hate the role of schemer, but now this opportunity had dropped into her lap, she had to make the most of it.

'What are you hiding?' Tadj demanded suspiciously.

He knew her too well. Even after so short a time, he could read her like a book. 'Nothing.' Guilt stabbed her.

'You seem tense to me,' he observed, clearly not convinced.

'If you'd give me an address, maybe I'd relax. I don't think you'd like to be in this position.'

'I wouldn't put myself in your position,' he assured her coldly. 'And, if I did, I wouldn't make a song and dance about it. I'd find a way out.'

He was distracted by a phone call, which left Lucy to gaze out of the window as Tadj spoke in Qalalan, and the limousine picked up speed as it moved seamlessly onto the Motorway.

'Are you ready to tell me what's on your mind?' he said when he cut the call. 'Perhaps an apology for walking out on me?' he suggested cuttingly. 'I get that you have a job, college and responsibilities. What I don't get is why you couldn't wake me before you left. My take is that you got what you wanted and had no more reason to stay.'

'What I wanted?' Lucy queried, frowning.

'Sex with the Emir,' Tadj derided. 'Was that something to brag about to your friends when you returned to the laundry? Or were you going to sell your story to the press?'

'Clearly not or everyone would know by now,' she said tensely, finding it harder every minute to stay cool.

Even as his face twisted with scorn, her heart squeezed tight to think of everything they'd lost. *Everything?* She *had* got what she wanted that night, but not in the way that Tadj imagined. The explosion of joy she'd experienced in his arms would stay with her all her life.

'I mistakenly thought we had something worth pursuing,' he said in the same cold tone. 'You slept in my arms, but when I woke you were gone. How do you expect me to trust you after that?'

'The way I felt about you frightened me,' she admitted bluntly.

'So you walked away,' he said with a disbelieving shake of his head.

'If I hadn't felt an instant connection, I wouldn't have trusted you enough to stay, let alone have sex with you.'

'I trusted *you.*'

He made it sound like an accusation. 'I wish we could start over,' Lucy admitted, longing for a return to the ease they'd enjoyed when they'd first met.

'I'm sure you do,' he agreed coldly.

'So why am I here, if you're so angry with me?'

'You mentioned a child?' he gritted out.

His tone was like a file, grinding her down…if she allowed it to. 'I never meant to mislead you. I was trying to be realistic, and didn't want either of us to regret what happened that night.'

The limousine slowed and Lucy realised they must

have reached their destination. She stared out of the window to see towering gates illuminated by powerful security lights, opening onto a long, wide drive. She felt increasingly isolated and uncertain as the limousine began its stately progress towards a large and extremely impressive house. An awe-inspiring sense of history surrounded the building that only emphasised the fact that this was Tadj's territory. But she was about to become a mother, the most fearsome warrior of all, and there was no chance she was going to fail her baby, or her mother.

Issues had always been black and white in the past, Tadj brooded as they approached the house, but that was pre-Lucy. Nothing was straightforward now. The depth of his feelings when he saw her in the restaurant had stunned him, as had the discovery that she was pregnant. What else was she hiding? Why should he believe anything she said now?

Yes, he had trust issues. Being abandoned as a child had left its mark, and he doubted his ability to trust could ever be rebuilt. But where Lucy was concerned, was it his pride at stake troubling him most? No woman had ever refused him, let alone walked out on him. No woman had ever moved him enough to care if she had. Doubt nagged at him. When their child was born, would she make a good mother, or would she desert the child as she'd deserted him? He'd believed Lucy to be different: unique, special. Was his judgement flawed? As the limousine approached the house, he remembered a woman in his youth telling him she loved him, before walking out with every portable treasure she could carry, as well as his overly generous loan for her so-called business.

Lucy had asked for nothing, and had taken nothing, other than a surprisingly large chunk of his stone-clad heart.

'Did I hurt you? Was I inconsiderate in any way? Was that why you didn't tell me about the baby?'

'No,' she exclaimed so forcefully he believed her. 'I couldn't get hold of you—no one on your staff would put me through.'

'You didn't try hard enough.'

'Maybe,' she conceded. 'But neither did I want you thinking I was after your support. For all I knew, you might have forgotten that night. And I couldn't put my life on hold for you,' she added, in a reminder that Lucy was no one's for the taking, but would have to be won.

A line of uniformed staff was waiting to greet them. Lucy tensed at his side. He felt some sympathy for her being catapulted into this very different world, and also some admiration for a woman who judged him as a man, not a king. Lucy's brutal honesty was good for him. It was her reluctance to share information he found irritating. It made him wonder what she was hiding. He would make it his business to find out. What could possibly be bigger news than the baby?

His thoughts were put on hold as the driver opened the door, and the formalities of the meet-and-greet began.

CHAPTER SEVEN

LOVE WAS HARD when it was all one-sided. Tadj's formal manner chilled her as he introduced Lucy to his staff. There was no easy path, and she couldn't help the way she felt about him. If love came with blame and guilt and pain, as well as aching loneliness when it ended, she'd take that, for a chance to be with him. And if only it were that straightforward, she thought as she returned the smiles of his staff.

The last member of staff to greet her was Tadj's house-keeper, who invited her inside the Emir of Qalala's beautiful country home, making Lucy feel so welcome she could almost believe this was more than an escape route for Lucy and a necessary pause for Tadj during which time he could soak in the startling fact that she was pregnant with his child and make plans accordingly.

She had just been shown into the library. Tadj was waiting in the huge and very beautiful book-lined room, where the scent of old leather and a roaring fire created a deceptively relaxed setting. Lucy perched on the edge of a sofa, while the housekeeper said she would order tea. When the door had closed behind her, Tadj lost no time making his intentions clear. This wasn't the fun guy from the café, but the Emir of Qalala claiming his prize. 'I've missed you,' he said. 'I believe we have un-finished business.'

His look scorched her, and with a million and one things she could have said—and maybe should have said—what came to her lips was, 'Yes…'

His big stride ate up the room, and within moments he had raised her to her feet. Cupping her face in his hands, he stared deep into her eyes as if he would know every secret in her heart.

With only the thin stuff of Lucy's red dress dividing them, he could feel her heart beating against his chest like the thrum of a hummingbird's wing.

'Nervous?' he queried softly. 'Or guilty?'

'Neither,' she assured him with the spirit he loved.

The sweep of her eyelashes created crescent shad-ows on her cheeks, making her even more beautiful, if such a thing were possible. She was young and vulner-able, and he should have known better, but when he was committed to a certain path he had never been known to change direction. He'd missed her more than he'd re-alised, and not just the sex, which, admittedly, had been astonishing. He'd missed Lucy—the essence of Lucy, and every little thing about her that made her unique. No other woman had ever come close, and nor would they. The royal marriage mart was a bank of tedium, full of women who held no appeal. At least, not for him. Who could after Lucy? But he'd always worked in the best in-terests of Qalala, and he always would, and a state mar-riage was just one more thing expected of him. Finding a *suitable* wife was—

'Stop,' Lucy gasped, pushing him away as he drove his mouth down on hers. 'You're kissing me as if this is your last day on earth. Why?' she asked, her green eyes full of what he believed to be genuine concern.

'You,' he said honestly. 'You drive me to the edge of reason.'

'Funny,' she said without a smile. 'I've thought the same about you. Truce?' she suggested.

Tempting, he thought. Nothing had changed since their first night together. He still wanted her, and Lucy's response to him said she felt the same. The initial shock of learning he was about to become the father to her unborn child was fading. They were consenting adults with no restrictions, and a loving mistress would always be better than a compliant wife. He kissed her again, this time tenderly, and as he caressed her face he was convinced that a dynamic relationship such as this was infinitely preferable to a negotiated marriage. Savouring their reunion was becoming easier by the moment. They were good together, and good for each other.

'Are you seducing me?' Lucy asked when finally he let her go. 'You're doing a pretty good job,' she told him before he had chance to answer.

Nothing fazed her. Lucy kept his feet on the ground, which was a big plus in her favour, especially when he recalled some of the over-indulged princesses who were paraded in front of him on a regular basis, so he could assess them as potential brides. 'You don't sound too unhappy about being seduced,' he observed.

'Maybe because I'm not.' Her low, sexy laugh vibrated through him. 'Just not here in the library while we're waiting for tea.' She gave a sharp cry of pleasure as he teased her by rasping his stubble just below her ear.

'So, don't scream too loud,' he advised. 'Would you like me to lock the door?' When it came to choosing between a mistress like Lucy and an obedient wife, Lucy made it no contest. His hunt for a wife could wait.

I've missed you so much it hurts, Lucy thought as Tadj brought her into his arms. Heartache, she had discovered, was a real, physical pain. Would it ease, or would it have been better if they'd never met again? For Tadj, she was certain the answer to that was yes, but she must leave the country, and he was her best, perhaps her only chance, so, while this was everything she needed and wanted, guilt reminded her that it was also a form of deceit in its way. This magnificent mansion with its history and elegant architecture only emphasised the fact that it was just a fraction of Tadj's global wealth. Whatever she did or said, when he found out she was using him to leave the country, he could only think she was after his money like all the rest.

'We'll be leaving for Qalala in the morning,' he said, distracting her with kisses.

'So soon.' She knew she should be glad, but, though they'd shared the greatest intimacy of all, they didn't know each other that well, and with every step it seemed she was leaving the familiar behind, and moving deeper into a world she didn't know.

'Don't look so worried,' he said, pulling back to stare into her face. 'You'll enjoy every privilege that comes with the position of official mistress.'

She gasped at the gulf between them, and Tadj's lack of understanding for how that statement made her feel. He couldn't have heard her, as he went on, 'I accept the term mistress might sound quaint to you, but it's all I've got.'

If that was meant to be funny, it missed its mark. 'Your whore, don't you mean?'

Tadj's expression changed in an instant. 'I'm sorry you

see it like that,' he said stiffly. He moved away from her, as if putting space between them would somehow help.

How else was she supposed to see it? Lucy wondered as a polite tap came on the door. 'That must be tea,' she said, realising how close she had come to spoiling her chance to escape the reach of her stepfather. She had a baby to think about now, as well as her mother. This wasn't all about her and what her pride would allow.

Standing up, she crossed the room and opened the door to admit the smiling housekeeper. She even surprised herself with her acting skills as she made space on a low table for the tray. 'Thank you. This is just what we need.' Any distraction would do, even when it came in the form of scones and jam.

'So, you agree to my proposal?' Tadj demanded the moment the door had closed behind his housekeeper.

'To become your mistress? I can't say it's my career goal. If I accompany you to Qalala, it will be because I want to.' *And because I need to*, Lucy silently admitted, feeling conflicted and wretched as she added distractedly, 'And because it will give us chance to decide on visitation rights.'

'Visitation rights?' Tadj exploded. 'This is the child of the Emir of Qalala you're talking about.'

She must calm things down. Everything depended on how she handled this. 'I'll come with you, not because of any so-called privileges, but because I choose to come for the good of the baby.' She drew a deep breath, relaxing a little, because that much was true. 'I'm quite capable of earning my own living.'

Tadj said nothing. He'd turned his attention to some documents on his desk. 'No tea,' he said curtly when she filled a cup and put it in front of him. 'You might as well go to your room.'

She was being dismissed like a child? 'Before I go, I need this address, as well as our address in Qalala. I need to let people know.'

'Qalala?' He glanced up briefly. 'The palace, of course.'

'Fair enough,' Lucy replied, carefully staying calm. 'But I can't just say "country house in the middle of no-where", can I?'

He was silent for so long, she thought he intended to ignore her. This was proving harder than she'd imagined, but if he thought she was a commodity to be traded be-tween countries and palaces at the Emir's convenience, he was about to discover he was wrong.

'Tadj, I—' Her jaw dropped when he picked up the phone and started talking in Qalalan. She was tempted to ask the housekeeper to call a cab so she could leave, but how would that help her baby and her mother?

'Address,' he said curtly after he'd ended his call. 'That is what you asked for, isn't it?' he demanded as he scrib-bled something down on a piece of paper. 'You've got everything you need from me now, I presume?'

If he thought that, Tadj really was a changed man.

'Call the friends and employers,' he insisted as he held out the phone. 'Tell your landlady you're safe with me. What else does she need to know?' he demanded when Lucy stood dumbstruck in front of him.

Perhaps it was hysteria, but she began to laugh. 'You don't know Miss Francine.' Lucy's landlady, the owner of the laundry where she worked, was noted for defending the women beneath her roof like a tigress with its cubs.

'Just tell her we're at my place in the Cotswolds, and reassure her that you're safe,' Tadj rapped impatiently.'

Safe? Lucy doubted she knew the meaning of the word. How would Tadj feel when he found out about her stepfather? Would she be safe then, or would she be prevented from seeing her child and sent home when he realised she had criminal connections? However big the risk, she had to do this, she decided as she placed the first call.

'Your decision about becoming my mistress?' Tadj prompted when her conversation ended, and they were waiting in tense silence for the housekeeper to knock on the door.

'Hasn't changed,' Lucy confirmed, still wondering if this aloof stranger was the same man she'd kissed, and with whom she'd shared such an explosion of joy when they'd made love. When they'd first met he'd seemed so humorous, and approachable, but now her hackles rose. 'How would you feel if I asked you to be my official lover?'

'Pretty good,' he said without missing a beat.

Not so aloof now, she thought, still feeling needled and demeaned by Tadj's suggestion. 'It's different,' she said, shaking her head. 'You're suggesting I become the Emir of Qalala's concubine. Do you know how cheap that makes me feel?'

That's your problem, his look suggested.

'Let's turn this on its head,' she said. 'I ask you to be my lover, making it clear that all I need from you is sex and laughs, with no expectations on either side. When I'm tired of you, I ditch you. I'd like to say I'd give you a pension when you leave, but I'm afraid that won't be possible.'

'Lucy!' Tadj rapped impatiently, 'That is not what I'm suggesting.'

'Well, it sounds like it,' she flared. 'Can't you see how ridiculous your suggestion is in this day and age? No,' she warned when his eyes flashed with humour. 'This isn't a joke. Don't mock me. I need you to take this seriously.'

She was full of angry frustration. No one could frustrate her like Tadj. She never knew if he was being serious or teasing her. The only certainty was that sensible Lucy was nowhere to be found when Tadj was in the frame.

Picking up the phone, Tadj spoke to the housekeeper, asking that she delay taking Lucy to her room for another half an hour. 'Sit down,' he said quietly when he'd cut the line. 'I have something to tell you—to explain to you.'

'Oh?' She took a couple of steadying breaths, which gave her enough time to accept that it might be to her advantage to listen.

'You think I'm being autocratic, but what you need to understand is that Qalala is different, and, though you're expecting my child, the position of mistress is the only way I can have that child recognised in some way.'

'In *some* way?' Lucy exclaimed with affront. 'That's not enough. Either you recognise your child or you don't. There can be no half measures where children are concerned.'

'Please hear me out.'

She agreed with a curt nod.

'Thank you.' Coming to sit on a chair facing her, Tadj explained, 'The constitution of Qalala only allows the Emir to make a constitutional marriage, which is always arranged by committee.'

'You're joking!' Lucy cut in with disbelief.

'Actually, I'm not,' Tadj said in the same measured tone. 'There were many things I wanted to change when I inherited the throne, but the first thing I had to do was to set Qalala back on its feet in order to stop my people starving. My uncle ruined the country, so I hope you can understand that those vital actions were much higher up my agenda than dealing with the country's antiquated laws. These laws also allow for the Emir to take concubines, as you call them, and further allows for their children to be recognised and accepted into society. I imagine the thinking was that these state-arranged marriages might not always succeed, and so a provision was put in place to allow future rulers to find some happiness with their mistresses and children.'

'Wow,' Lucy murmured, utterly lost for words.

They were both silent for quite a while; now Tadj had been so frank with her, she felt she owed the same to him. 'Seems we both have something to confess,' she admitted.

As they stared at each other, she could see that Tadj was wondering what new bombshell was about to hit. Better to speak frankly, and hold nothing back. 'I need to get out of the country fast,' she admitted.

Tadj's expression didn't change, so, inhaling shakily, she told him the rest. 'My stepfather is a criminal and has just been released from jail.'

She expected a reaction, but Tadj's face told her nothing. 'He's a criminal boss with a very long reach, who made my mother's life a misery, and now he's threatening my mother through me. If she doesn't take him back, he'll come after me. That's why my mother begged me to get out of the country. I received the call from her quite literally minutes before I saw you in the restaurant. You gave me the perfect way out,' she admitted. 'So, there you are,' she said when Tadj remained silent. 'I need you to help me, and you want me to be your mistress, so your child will be recognised and not hidden away. If a compromise is possible, I have to consider it…' she waited. 'Please say something.'

Tadj picked up the phone 'I'm calling my housekeeper to show you to your room. Be ready to leave for Qalala first thing in the morning.'

CHAPTER EIGHT

LUCY GOT HER chance to call both her employers while
Tadj was speaking to his housekeeper about the latest arrangements. Her second and most important call was to
Miss Francine, a woman she had really come to care for.
As she stood in the baronial hallway, she frowned as she
waited for her elderly friend to pick up, thinking how to
frame her news. She didn't want to cause any alarm, so
it was crucial to find the right words. Tadj's suggestion
that Lucy should become his official mistress was enough
to send anyone into a tailspin, let alone a kindly octoge-
narian. As the log fire crackled, and the phone trilled in
her ear, Lucy's thoughts returned to Tadj. Could a man
insensitive enough to ask her to become his mistress
in this day and age be expected to make a good father?

She didn't get the chance to progress the thought, and
had to swiftly rejig her thoughts when Miss Francine answered. Having explained where she was and who she
was with, Lucy explained that the Emir of Qalala had
invited her to visit his country with a view to putting
on an exhibition of the famous sapphires. It was almost
the truth, and it was a relief when an excited Miss Francine took over from there. She'd read about the Sapphire
Sheikhs, and believed the trip to Qalala to see the sap-

phire mines with an opportunity to display would make a wonderful addition to Lucy's CV. She chatted about Lucy's college course, and remembered that Lucy had always excelled at displaying various exhibits to their best advantage.

'Take all the time you need,' Miss Francine enthused. 'This is too good an opportunity for you to miss.'

That was one way of putting it, but then Lucy hadn't mentioned the complications. 'See you soon,' she said fondly as they ended the call.

'Maybe not so soon.'

She spun around to find Tadj standing behind her. 'Were you eavesdropping on my conversation?'

'No more than you're abusing your position as guest in my home.'

'I'm sorry—by doing what?' Lucy enquired.

'By talking about me as if I weren't here.'

'Well, you weren't here,' she said. 'And that's rich coming from the man who just invited me to become his mistress.'

Within moments, the battle lines were drawn. Emotions were running high between them, which was no surprise, Lucy conceded, when so much had happened in so short a time. If only there could be more than this, she thought as they stared at each other unblinking. The trip to Qalala was more than she could have wished for, but even that was tainted by the way it had been achieved. She hated this devious game-playing, when all she wanted was an honest relationship.

Between the Emir of Qalala and Lucy Gillingham? Dream on!

It was a relief to see the smiling housekeeper, ready to escort Lucy to her room.

'Mrs Brown will take good care of you,' Tadj said in a neutral tone that suggested Lucy was just another guest in his house. When did he plan the big reveal? she wondered.

'You'll find clothes in the dressing room in your suite,' he added in the same emotion-free tone. 'We'll meet later when you've had a chance to freshen up.'

For a trial run? Lucy's expression suggested coolly.

The housekeeper hadn't noticed, and was already heading across the hall. Tadj's mention of clothes in Lucy's dressing room made her think that he'd had this all planned out; whatever she'd said about becoming his mistress, his decision had been made. A chill ran through her at the thought that, once again, Tadj was in charge. He always had been in charge from the moment they'd met again in the restaurant, she accepted tensely.

'I expect to see you back in the library in one hour's time,' he called after her as he jogged up the stairs. She took his harsh tone of voice as more proof that the fun, uncomplicated man she'd met in a café had disappeared completely.

'You wouldn't be the first to stand and gaze around in wonder at all the treasures here,' the housekeeper said, misreading Lucy's expression. 'And I doubt you'll be the last,' she added with an encouraging smile.

'It's so beautiful here,' Lucy admitted, glad of the change of subject, taking in the stained-glass windows as they mounted the stairs, and intricate carvings on the bannisters and over the doors. 'I've never seen anything like this, except in stately homes that are open to the public.'

'The Emir is a very particular man,' Mrs Brown told her as she led the way.

So, where do I fit in? Lucy wondered. Furnishings, paintings, and more space than one man could ever use, even with a full team of staff, made her feel increasingly superfluous as Mrs Brown led her deeper into the wolf of Qalala's lair. Even the air smelled of money, though it was impossible to fault the restrained and classy décor. Deep-piled carpet soaked up their footsteps, while framed photographs made her pause and finally accept that this fabulous place was actually a home. Home to a very rich man, Lucy concluded, spotting a particularly striking image of Tadj, coated in mud after a polo match. Even in that shot, he looked amazing.

She stopped in front of another framed photograph, showing him seated on rough wooden benches. She assumed this must have been taken at the sapphire mine. Surrounded by working men, he appeared as one of them, relaxed and at home, in dust-covered jeans and a ripped top, his face streaked with dirt. The photographer had caught him in a pose with his arms outstretched to encompass the men on either side of him, and they were all smiling. How she longed to have that uncomplicated relationship. She could feel the warmth between them, even through the impartial medium of a camera. If only she could see more of that side of him, she thought as Mrs Brown led the way. They had reached a broad, light-filled corridor, where one more framed shot made her pause. This one was of Tadj with his friend Sheikh Khalid. Both men were grinning with pleasure, as well they might, as they were holding up handfuls of the biggest sapphires she'd ever seen.

'That photograph was taken in Qalala,' Mrs Brown explained when she noticed Lucy's interest. 'His Serene Majesty loves anything that reminds him of his friends and his homeland. Have you been to Qalala? It's very beautiful.'

As beautiful as here? Lucy wondered as she admired the craftsmanship around her that gave such a sense of history, of destiny.

'His Majesty treats his staff to a holiday in Qalala each year,' Mrs Brown continued as she walked on. 'His Majesty is so generous.'

And so distant from me, Lucy thought with regret as Mrs Brown paused in front of a highly polished mahogany door. 'It's no surprise people love him as they do,' Tadj's adoring housekeeper went on. 'You'll have a wonderful time when you go to Qalala—and I feel sure the Qalalan people will love you.'

'Oh, but I'm not—'

Too late. Mrs Brown had already entered the room, leaving Lucy to wonder if she'd been mistaken for more than she was. She couldn't imagine the Emir's official mistress had much of a public role, but what did she know?

A small yet luxuriously carpeted and decorated lobby promised a more than comfortable overnight stay at least. On top of a gilt and marble console table, one more photograph claimed Lucy's interest.

Mrs Brown heaved a sigh when she saw Lucy looking at it. 'His Serene Majesty asked me not to put so many photographs about, but I think it makes the place look homely.'

'I agree,' Lucy said politely, but with a warm smile for Mrs Brown. There was nothing remotely homely about the man in the photograph. Tadj sat astride a richly caparisoned black stallion. Wearing traditional robes, with his head and face partially concealed behind a flowing black headdress, he looked more like a formidable conqueror who took no prisoners than the genial employer Mrs Brown had described, though the housekeeper's opinion of her regal employer was to Tadj's credit, Lucy conceded. She would have known him anywhere. His eyes were unmistakeable, as were his bearing and uncompromising pose. A shiver of awareness ran down her spine as it occurred to her that Tadj might not be prepared to compromise in any way at all when it came to discussing the future of their child.

'Where does this door lead?' she asked to distract herself from such a troubling thought.

'It's a connecting door to His Majesty's suite,' Mrs Brown explained. 'You can leave it locked, if you prefer, or open the door, if that suits you better.'

Delicately put, Lucy thought. 'I see.' She did see, and, though she might have stepped out of her world and into his, the door between them would remain firmly locked.

As soon as Mrs Brown had left Lucy to her own devices, she decided to freshen up first, and then change her clothes before going down to the library. Stripping off, she donned a robe, ready to take a shower before exploring her dressing room. She loved everything about her accommodation, especially the outlook over the lake. A lake…imagine that, she mused. This had to be one of the most beautiful and fabulous houses in the country. She found the pink marble bathroom and stripped off. After a moment or two of awestruck stillness, she ran the shower in a space that would easily accommodate a rugby team, and stepped beneath the warm, soothing water. She actually felt her shoulders sag as the tension dropped out of them. Bliss, she mused happily, relaxing for the first time since her shock encounter with Tadj in the restaurant. Closing her eyes, she lifted her face to the warm, refreshing spray. And then heard an unmistakeable footstep.

'*Tadj!*' She spun around on her heels as he joined her in the steamy cubicle. He was stark naked too. 'You've got a nerve,' she exclaimed as her heart threatened to beat its way out of her chest.

'Don't I,' he agreed.

Powered by surprise, she pressed her hands against his chest. Tadj was rock hard, and didn't move. Tadj, hot, wet and hard, was enough to melt the firmest resolve. Animal instinct took over. Anger was a passion, and passion led to lust. They'd been too long apart, and she'd missed him too much. All they'd shared was too fresh in her memory. Yanking her close, he held her firmly against his hard length and kissed her, and within moments she was kissing him back.

There was no point trying to pretend she didn't want this. Pressed up against him with those skilful hands resting on her buttocks, she could only think of one thing. But it pleased her to put up a token struggle, just for the friction of his body against hers.

'Are you saying you don't want this?' he demanded harshly. Dipping at the knees, he teased her in the way she loved.

'Tadj...'

'Yes?' he murmured, knowing she would soon be past speech.

'What are you doing?' she gasped, wanting to delay the moment of mating to make it all the sweeter.

'Water saving?' Tadj's lips pressed down with irony. 'Auditioning for my new role as your lover?'

No need for that, she thought. She wanted to say,

'Hurry,' but refused to give him the satisfaction. And this was Tadj, the man she loved, the man she would always love. 'In your own time,' she said, matching his cynical tone.

He was on fire for her. She was perfection beneath his hands. Every curve of her body might have been designed with him in mind. He might be bigger than she was, but they fitted together perfectly. She matched him in every way there was. Right now, it was her breasts claiming his attention. When he caressed them, her nipples pressed imperatively against his palms. Lucy was all heat. Her familiar wildflower scent intoxicated his senses. Slipping his hands beneath her buttocks, he positioned her, while she gripped his arms as if her life depended on it. The desire to possess her grew stronger with every passing second, as did his wish for the novelty of serving—for now—as her all too willing lover. He was so turned on he was in agony. Remembering the last time they'd had sex didn't help, because it reminded him how big he was, how tight she was, and how it felt to be deep inside her. It was also a timely reminder to take things slowly so he didn't hurt her.

This consideration went no way to discouraging Lucy, who commanded, 'No, don't take your hand away. I like it where it is. If you're my lover, you have to do as I wish, which means following my commands to the letter.'

This was one instruction he had no difficulty obeying, and he laughed softly to see her reaction as he stimulated her the way she liked. 'I'm yours to command,' he said as he thrust her up against the wall. She wrapped her legs around him as he lifted her, and, with water cascading over them, he gave her what she wanted.

Some things would always overrule common sense,

and even pride, Lucy thought as Tadj brought her to the edge of reason, and this was one of them. As she rocketed into the first noisy release, she had to accept that she needed this—him—so badly that she wouldn't be able to think straight until he'd done with her. It was a long time before she quieted, then she realised groggily that Tadj was still kissing her, still moving, as he awakened her to the possibility of more pleasure.

'How did I do?' he asked dryly. 'Do I get the job?'

'I haven't decided yet,' she lied, smiling against his chest. She felt so safe in Tadj's embrace, she never wanted to move—never wanted this to end, but it would end; it must, because Tadj was the Emir of Qalala, while she was an independent woman, building her life and career, who had no intention of throwing everything away on a passion that must surely burn itself out. Becoming his mistress was a short-term arrangement, while being a mother was for life. She must remain free and self-sufficient, though it was all too easy to think they were meant to be together. Reality was harsh, she accepted as he nuzzled her neck and prepared to take her again. Tadj's life would move on, as would hers. 'No,' she whispered.

'No, until Qalala?' he suggested, the same irony colouring his tone, as if he doubted restraint was possible. 'You do well to conserve your strength.'

'I'm looking forward to visiting your country,' she said honestly, 'but I'm making one condition.'

Tadj's brows shot up. 'Which is?' he pressed.

'That no announcement is made about my becoming your official mistress.'

Tadj's expression darkened. No one had ever given the Emir of Qalala instructions before, Lucy presumed.

'You need to get away, don't you?'

'Yes,' she readily accepted, 'but I think more of you than to think you mean to hold me to ransom for that. I have a life, Tadj, as you do—Tadj, no!' she insisted as he dipped at the knees to take her again.

'Tadj, yes,' he argued in a soft, husky tone that tormented her senses to the point of no return.

'I need you to take me seriously,' she managed somehow to gasp out.

'Oh, I do,' he assured her as he did what they both needed, and with the most consummate skill.

CHAPTER NINE

IT WAS HARD to remain unmoved when you loved someone as much as she loved Tadj, Lucy realised as they kissed and touched. She felt safe in his arms as Tadj took her on a journey of pleasure; he made her forget everything, except arousal, which he increased by murmuring words in his own tongue. Even fears of the inevitable emotional fallout when this love affair ended, as it surely must when he returned to being the Emir of Qalala, and she was a working mother, stood no chance.

'Not done yet?' he whispered when she tried to steady her emotion-fuelled breathing. 'Then, use me as you want,' he invited.

'No energy left. You drained me completely.'

'I don't believe you.'

Tadj's darkly amused expression worked its magic, and she reached for him again, with the warning, 'You'll have to do all the work.'

'As your official lover, I expect to. It's my duty,' he said dryly.

'I'm glad you understand your responsibilities,' she agreed, longing for so much more. But Tadj was too good for her to ignore the sensation building inside her, and she groaned to encourage him as he continued. He brought her to the edge quickly, but kept her waiting, leaving her stranded on a plateau of pleasure, from which there seemed no way down. 'Please,' she begged.

'No,' he said flatly. 'In my own time, I seem to remember you instructing.'

He hissed through his teeth as Lucy reached for him. Had he forgotten that her appetite matched his? He took her again, firmly, slamming her against the wall as he dipped at the knees to thrust deep.

'Yes, yes! Please!' she responded in a throaty scream.

'I aim to please,' he said, relishing how tight she was as he set up a firm and regular beat.

'You *do* please,' she assured him, laughing with abandon as she moved vigorously in time with him.

He brought her to the edge and tipped her over, not once, but several times, until he was sure the marble must crack under the force of her screams of pleasure. When finally she lay quiet and relaxed in his arms, he swaddled her in a warm, fluffy towel and carried her to bed, where they made love again.

It was dark when Lucy finally surfaced, feeling very well used and as contented as a kitten.

Wake up! She was no kitten. Allowing her feelings for Tadj to grow was reckless. Giving herself body and soul, when nothing in the future was certain, was just building more trouble.

Stirring, he turned to look at her, hugging her knees and resting her chin on them as she brooded. 'Changing your mind about coming to Qalala with me?' he suggested. 'If you are I'll change it back again.'

Once more couldn't hurt, her body insisted as it overruled Lucy's sensible mind.

The next time she woke, daylight was streaming into

the room, and the bed beside her was empty. Turning her face into the pillows, she heaved a contented sigh and inhaled Tadj's warm, clean man scent. He must be in the shower, she thought. Sitting up, she grabbed a robe, and prepared to go exploring. The connecting door between their respective suites was open, and she could hear water splashing against the marble tiles. She pulled back on the thought that it was better to prepare for the day ahead than invade Tadj's shower, as he had invaded hers. She'd never be ready to leave if she joined him.

As uncomfortable as she felt rifling through all the high-end designer goods in the sumptuously fitted-out dressing room, she had to find something to wear. She settled on a simple outfit of trousers, shirt, and a sweater, then slipped her feet into the softest leather moccasins she had ever worn. They fitted perfectly. Everything fitted perfectly. Tadj had mapped her body with consummate skill, and whoever had gone shopping for him had the same understated taste as Lucy. The exclusive lingerie was the only exception to this rule as it was composed of the finest silk and lace, and far better suited to the mistress of the Emir than a casual guest, Lucy thought as she held up the flimsy garments, only to see light flooding through them. They were lovely and luxurious, but once again it seemed that Tadj was in control. How much stronger would his rule over her become in Qalala? There had to be a way to restore some balance between them, and it was up to Lucy to find it.

There were so many cosmetics, all brand new in their original boxes. It was as if the same person who'd bought the clothes had visited a high-end store and bought up every shade and product on the counter. Ignoring most of it, she drew a brush through her hair and slicked on some lip gloss. Carefully rolling up her red dress, she put it in a laundry bag to take with her. Leaving the suite, she found her way downstairs to breakfast by following the sound of clinking plates.

'Good morning.' Her heart flipped over as Tadj lifted his head as she walked into the light-filled room.

'Good morning,' she replied, trying to act cool, when his look was full of heat, and his husky tone was all it took to make her want him again.

'May I pour you some coffee?' he asked politely.

'That would be nice. Thank you,' she said.

Pausing for a moment in front of the floor-to-ceiling glass walls in the breakfast room, she admired the exquisitely designed gardens. The morning room was decorated in subtle shades that echoed the scene outside. Beyond the gardens, a lake as placid as a plate was home to swans that cruised in a stately white armada. She tore her gaze away as a hovering attendant pulled out a chair at the dining table. The unreality of the situation struck her forcibly as she sat down. Well, that was no wonder when she lived in a bedsit, and her usual breakfast was a rushed mug of instant coffee and a bowl of cereal, Lucy concluded with her customary good humour.

And then there was Tadj.

With his brutally muscular frame, and swarthy complexion, he didn't belong in these refined surroundings any more than she did, Lucy thought, until she remembered he was a desert king.

'I forgive you for sleeping through,' he said as the attendants came forward to offer Lucy countless selections from many different platters of food, 'but my flight plan is non-negotiable,' he added in a curt tone as soon as they were alone. 'We leave immediately after you finish breakfast.'

Should she bolt it down?

'No longer than half an hour,' he instructed.

Now the moment had come and her departure to Qalala was imminent, Lucy had to remind herself of all the reasons why this trip was necessary. Even so, she couldn't shake the feeling that she was jumping out of the frying pan and into the fire.

'Your clothes are being packed as we speak,' Tadj went on, 'so there's no need for you to rush your breakfast.'

'But—'

A single word was all he gave her chance to say before he left the room.

Sinking down in her chair again, Lucy reviewed her options. There were none. She was on holiday from college and had made calls to both her employers, so there was no reason why she couldn't go to Qalala. Apart from any advantage to Lucy and her CV, as Miss Francine had put it, there was a far more important reason to visit Tadj's homeland. Qalala was the other half of her baby's heritage, and Lucy owed it to her child to know something about the country. On top of that, the chance to be with Tadj and see the land he loved through his eyes would tell her more than anything about Qalala, and about the man she loved. Whether he would agree to be her guide, she supposed, would depend on whether she asked the question of the Emir of Qalala, or the man she knew as Tadj.

He was piloting the jet, so there was little chance for him to interface with Lucy. What? *Interface?* To be with her? To drink her in? To inhale and enjoy her familiar warmth and scent. He wanted Lucy more than he could safely express, though after what he'd learned about her past and Lucy's so-called family life, he doubted she would ever be completely open with him. She wasn't completely open with anyone. What was it about Lucy that took up every available space in his brain? She tested his so far unchallenged belief in his own judgement. Her stubbornness angered and frustrated him in equal measure.

He was accustomed to controlling every situation and should cut her some slack, he concluded. Lucy trod her own path, because she'd had to, and was as intent on doing the right thing, as she saw it, as he was.

Missing her had nagged at him every day they'd been apart. Even now, seated in the comfortable area behind the cockpit, she wasn't nearly close enough. He was impatient to introduce her to Qalala, so she could understand why he loved it so much. He was impatient to see the country through her eyes. Making her feel comfortable in the desert was the first step to installing her as his mistress. The constitution of Qalala allowed for nothing more. And he wasn't about to let Lucy and his child slip through his fingers.

Lucy might be everything he looked for in a mistress, he accepted with a grim smile as he prepared to hand over control of the jet to his first officer, but she still seemed to need convincing of that.

'Take over, will you?' he asked his first officer.

It was a long flight to Qalala, which was an opportunity to further explain to Lucy that an official mistress in Qalala enjoyed the same freedoms and privileges as a wife. Slanting a grim smile, he expected his formidable powers of persuasion to be put to their sternest test yet.

'Tadj…' Lucy smiled as he approached, as if she was

pleased to see him, which was surprising considering he'd been so abrupt with her this morning. She had her own games to play.

'My apologies. I was in a hurry this morning to make plans for our arrival.'

'Oh,' she said blandly with the faintest of smiles.

If he'd stayed any longer in the breakfast room, he would have dismissed the attendants and had her on the table, and that would definitely have delayed their departure.

'I thought you were flying this thing,' she said as he settled down on the seat next to her.

'This *thing* flies itself,' he assured her, 'and, of course, there's a first officer as well as an engineer on deck.'

'What if there's an emergency?' she demanded, cocking her chin to challenge him with this.

'My first officer is a fully qualified pilot. I'm sure he can handle things.'

'I'd prefer it if you were in charge.'

'Really?' He huffed a grim smile. 'Should I be flattered by this sudden reversal in your opinion?'

'Only if you're desperate,' she said.

They were back to the teasing banter. Good, that worked in his favour. Things would be so much easier if they were back on good terms.

'Stop frowning. My first officer will make sure we stay on course.'

'Are *we* back on course?' she countered fast.

'Shall we?' Losing no time to conversation, he jerked his chin towards the rear of the aircraft.

She stared at him for a moment and then left her seat.

'I have a suite of rooms at the back,' he explained as he led the way aft.

'Of course you do,' Lucy murmured with amusement.

'And a private study,' he informed her, 'as well as a rather comfortable bedroom, a sitting room, and a screening room—it's up to you.'

'The study?' she said.

'For a serious discussion?' he suggested.

'Absolutely,' she confirmed.

He'd had something else in mind, but if he learned more about Lucy's experience of her stepfather, it would be useful, not to mention that a part of him was very disturbed by Lucy's fear of the man. He also needed to reassure Lucy that as long as she was under his protection—and what greater protection could he offer than to make her his mistress?—she had nothing, and no one, to fear. And that protection would naturally extend to her mother. He'd had the man checked out, of course, but first-hand information was always welcome.

He opened the door on an informal and very comfortable seating area.

'This is your study?'

He indicated the desk. 'Relaxation as well as my business needs are provided for here. Take a seat,' he invited.

She had everything she wanted to say to Tadj set out in her mind, and it would be a relief to fill in the gaps, but as she dredged up facts about her stepfather she thought Tadj should know about, she was frustrated to notice her hands were shaking.

'That bad,' Tadj murmured as he propped a hip against the desk.

'You have no idea,' she admitted, knowing that they were on the same wavelength as always.

'I have some,' he said.

Dipping his chin, he left a space for her to fill, so she

told him everything: the violence, the fear, her stepfather's unexpected release from prison that had left her mother so vulnerable.

'She's in a refuge now,' Tadj stated calmly.

'How do you know?' she asked with surprise.

'With guards who'll look out for her,' he added. 'She'll come to no harm. I can promise you that.'

There was a tense silence as Lucy took this in, and then she guessed softly, 'Your guards are looking after her.'

'You didn't expect me to sit on the information and do nothing, did you? Your mother will be transferred safely to her own home as soon as I receive confirmation that your stepfather, who broke a court order to approach and threaten your mother, and, through her, you, is back in jail where he belongs.'

Lucy's mouth worked as she tried to take this in, but no words came out, until at last she admitted, 'I don't know what to say.'

'Don't say anything. Bullies have to be dealt with, and I'm lucky enough to have the resources to enable me to do that.'

'Thank you.' It didn't seem enough, when what Tadj had done without seeking any thanks at all had almost certainly saved her mother's life.

'No thanks are necessary,' he said in the same even tone. 'And now you're safe too,' he added.

And massively in debt to Tadj, whom she loved and believed she was starting to know. Tadj's brain was rigidly compartmentalised with the biggest section devoted to duty to his country and its people, and the next devoted to justice. He would never break the laws of Qalala, which left Lucy finely balanced between self-determination and gratitude. Needing time and space to think, she stood.

'Sit,' he insisted.

'I'd rather stand, if you don't mind.'

'And even if I do, I'm guessing,' he suggested dryly.

He towered over her, all-powerful and compelling, making her wish she had sketch pad handy to record the moment that Lucy Gillingham confronted the Emir of Qalala.

'You've been through a lot,' he said.

'So have many people.' Tipping her chin, she stared him in the eyes. 'The fact that we both have should make it easier to talk about the future of our child.'

Tadj made no reply, but this was a good place for them to talk, as there was no escape, Lucy thought. 'In six months time we'll be parents, responsible for a new life. I'm thrilled. I hope you are?'

'You want to know how I feel about becoming a father?' Tadj said in a voice she couldn't read. 'Ecstatic? Is that what you want to hear?'

Was this the Emir of Qalala or Tadj speaking? Lucy's emotions were so messed up, she couldn't tell. All she knew was that they were at an impasse with no tidy answers, and no way she could think of to make this right. There was only one constant, Lucy concluded as she folded her hands protectively over her stomach. She loved this man, and would always love him, and she grieved for the fact that they couldn't be like other couples, and share equally in this greatest joy of all.

CHAPTER TEN

HE WAS ECSTATIC at the thought of becoming a father, but there remained a lot for them to set in place to protect those he cared about. Lucy's expression was wounded. She didn't know what to expect of him. Perhaps that was for the best. He still had many facts and consequences to absorb and consider. The days of keeping royal lives private were long past, which was a good thing, in his opinion, and an idea was already starting to take shape in his mind.

'It's a long flight,' he said factually, 'and I think you should take advantage of the bedrooms on board.'

Was that an order, or an invitation? Lucy wondered as she rose to her feet.

'You mentioned we'd be staying in a palace in Qalala? I wasn't sure which one,' she admitted. 'I didn't realise you owned so many. I really should tell Miss Francine which one I'm staying in to reassure her...'

Tadj shrugged. 'We'll be visiting my fort in the desert. It isn't a prison,' he added when Lucy pulled a face, 'but a building of historic importance that has been completely renovated and refurbished, and I now consider it to be one of my most luxurious and well-equipped homes. Architects and historians worldwide seem to agree with me, as Wolf Fort has recently been designated one of the wonders of both the modern and the ancient world. I always find a stay there refreshing, and I'm sure you will too. It will give you chance to rest as you absorb another part of your baby's heritage.'

'Our baby,' Lucy said. 'Sounds great, but now, if you don't mind, I'd like to lie down…if someone would be good enough to show me to my bedroom.'

She was mentally exhausted and emotionally drained, Lucy concluded as Tadj picked up the phone, but at least everything was out in the open.

'One of the flight attendants will show you the way,' Tadj said coolly. 'I'll make sure you're woken up before we land.'

A moment of pure panic hit, when she realised that the Emir of Qalala could arrange for her to be hustled off the plane and locked away until she had her baby. She'd taken so much on trust, Lucy thought as she snatched a look over her shoulder to see if anything of the guy in the café remained.

'Go,' he said, glancing up from the documents he'd been studying. 'You look exhausted.'

Had she lost his trust along the way? She could only hope not. If this was it, and they could never be close again, there would be a big black hole in her life that nothing could fill.

The bedroom on board Tadj's jet was quite small but well equipped with the most comfortable bed, Lucy thought with a relieved sigh as she settled down on the crisp white sheets. But sleep didn't come easily, and she tossed and turned as she tried to work out what Tadj was thinking. When she finally drifted off to sleep there were worry lines between her brows, but she slept heavily, only waking when the promised knock came on the door.

Having taken a fast shower, she wrapped a towel around her and came out to find fresh clothes laid out on the bed. It was pretty much a replay of the clothes she'd been wearing when she boarded the aircraft. Who'd done this for her? she wondered, tracing the edge of the fabric with her fingers. Time to get her head around the fact that billionaires lived very different lives, with squads of people to anticipate their every need. The engine noise was already changing in preparation for landing, and with a shrug she pulled on the clothes.

Back in the main cabin, there was no sign of Tadj. He must have returned to the flight deck to take over the landing of the plane. She took her seat, and as the undercarriage went down she felt safe in his hands. Outside the window, a spectacular light show of pink, indigo, and gold was the most spectacular welcome to Qalala. The jet was on its final approach to what appeared to be a solitary airstrip in rolling miles of golden desert. By the time the wheels touched down, the purple light of dusk had settled over the land, but far from this being a sinister, or isolated location, Lucy could see vast crowds had gathered. The length of the runway was lined with bonfires, and people were already celebrating Tadj's return. Entire families seemed to have turned out to welcome him home. There were even riders on horseback, dressed in traditional robes, waving flambeaux in the air. The Emir of Qalala was home.

'Are you ready to disembark?'

Lucy turned to see Tadj standing behind her in the aisle. For a moment words escaped her. No more the conventionally dressed pilot, but in traditional black robes edged with gold, and a flowing black headdress wrapped around his head and face. The air of danger and exoticism he exuded was phenomenal. The photograph in his country house did him no justice at all.

'Lucy?' he prompted when she didn't move right away. 'People are waiting for us.'

Tempted to stubbornly refuse to rush, she remembered the countless people who had waited so long to greet their ruler, so she did rush, and was greeted on exit by warm gusts of spice-laden air, mixed with the astringent tang of aviation fuel.

'Shouldn't you go first?' she asked Tadj when he indicated that she should go ahead of him.

A flight attendant discreetly explained that the Emir would exit the aircraft last, which seemed strange to Lucy, but she didn't want to tread on any toes at such an early stage of the visit. Stepping out, she was blinded by lights, all of which were directed at the small platform at the top of the aircraft steps. She was just one of many being used to dress the stage, she realised, before the star of the show made his appearance. The cheers were deafening as the Emir of Qalala dipped his head to exit the jet. As he stepped out into the light his name was chanted repeatedly. With the sound vibrating through her body, Lucy had to remind herself that this man was the father of her child.

After descending the steps and greeting the official welcoming party, Tadj strode away towards the first in a fleet of sleek black SUVs. Lucy wondered if everyone who followed her onto the runway was heading to Wolf Fort.

Tadj's off-roader sped off before Lucy had chance to work out which SUV she was supposed to be travelling in. She had never felt more isolated than she did now, amongst this crowd of strangers, all of whom seemed to know exactly where they were heading. The sense of unreality only intensified as a gust of wind blew desert sand into her eyes. Everyone else was wearing protective headgear, she noticed. For once, it was a relief when a black-clad security guard, in a sharp suit, with a suspicious bulge beneath his jacket, ushered her towards one of the SUVs.

If only Tadj could have given her a few words of reassurance and explained what was happening.

Was this how he had felt three months ago?

Chastened, she climbed into the vehicle. No longer the lover, Tadj was the Emir of Qalala, and she would be a fool to forget it. She might be the mother of his child, but her future in this foreign land was unknowable and uncertain.

They'd driven for miles in the dark, sometimes on the highway, and sometimes on bumpy tracks, when suddenly lights appeared in the distance, and the ghostlike walls of an imposing edifice loomed out of the shadows. The fort was brilliantly lit and didn't appear sinister at all. Flags were flying in celebration of the Emir's return, and fireworks lit up the sky. Lucy's anxiety was quickly replaced by avid curiosity, and as the vehicle slowed to a halt she could see the official party greeting Tadj on the steps of the fortress. Everyone was dressed in the flowing robes of Qalala, and a guard of honour lined the route across a vast courtyard to an imposing stone entrance beyond. It was a disappointment to see Tadj disappear inside the ancient walls, but an elderly man who had stepped forward to greet her introduced himself as Abdullah as he bowed over her hand, and greeted her with warmth, saying politely, 'Welcome to Qalala. I hope you have had a good journey? As soon as I have seen you comfortably settled in your suite of rooms, I will take your order for food and drink, and hand over the agenda for your stay.'

'My agenda?' Lucy queried.

'His Majesty is leaving for the sapphire mines in the morning, and expects you to join him.'

Why couldn't Tadj tell her that? 'The sapphire mines?' she prompted, to the echoing clatter of their feet on the stone-paved courtyard. 'Are the mines far away?'

'No more than a day's ride,' Abdullah informed her with a gentle and reassuring smile. Bowing politely once more, he invited Lucy to go ahead of him into Wolf Fort.

Of course Tadj was busy, Lucy reasoned. He'd only just arrived home. She must be patient. But why did he want her to see the mines? Her surroundings distracted her. The historic fort was stunning and atmospheric, and called for more than one sketch to record this perfect blend of old and new. Behind its towering exterior, she found every modern luxury, even an elevator to transport her to her accommodation, which, it amused Lucy to find, was in a turret. If this was to be her home for the next unspecified number of days, Lucy thought as she turned full circle, it was going to be a magical stay, and she had the additional reassurance of knowing that her stepfather would never find her here.

'Do you like it?' Abdullah asked as she took in the fantasia of silk hangings, jewel-coloured rugs, and gilded mirrors.

'I love it,' Lucy enthused. 'Please thank the Emir for his kindness in allowing me to stay here, as well as all the staff who've prepared so thoughtfully for my arrival.' She was looking at the colourful exotic floral displays, the platters of delicious fruits, and jugs of squeezed juices. The turret suite was an unusual space with curving rough stone walls. These were softened by colourful and tasteful decorations, and beyond the windows she could see the crenellated battlements dressed for the Emir's return with a forest of flags.

'Your agenda, Miss Gillingham…'

Lucy turned in time to see Abdullah placing a document on top of a gilded console table. 'And your menu for tonight,' he added, placing a second sheet of paper on top of the first. 'Though, of course, the kitchen will accommodate anything you care for, and at any time you'd like to eat it.' His face broke into a smile, as if it delighted him to share the pleasures of the fort with Lucy.

'A chicken wrap?' she asked, mouth already watering at the thought as she returned his smile. Pregnancy cravings could pop up at the most unlikely times.

'With extra fries?' Abdullah anticipated with a grin.

'Wonderful,' Lucy enthused, relaxing for the first time since arriving in Qalala. 'Before you go,' she added as he turned to go, 'does His Majesty have a direct line?' She was done with hanging around, leaving the rest of her stay in the hands of fate and the Emir of Qalala.

'Didn't His Majesty write it down for you?'

If she told the truth, that Tadj hadn't offered to give Lucy his private number, she could be stranded in the turret until morning. 'I'm sure he meant to,' she said, 'but in the rush of coming here…'

'Of course…' Pulling out a pen from the pocket of his robe with a flourish, her gallant escort wrote Tadj's number on the top of her agenda.

The door had barely closed behind him when Lucy

pounced on the piece of paper. Reading the item immediately below the telephone number, she saw that she should be ready to leave by helicopter for the sapphire mines at dawn. She wanted to speak to Tadj before then. The tension of not knowing how he really felt about the baby was tearing her up inside. But his phone rang out. She tried three times and could only conclude that he'd decided not to take her calls. He was busy, she reminded herself firmly.

Pregnancy hormones had a lot to answer for, Lucy concluded when she paced up and down until she couldn't resist calling him one last time. After another fail, she flung the phone onto the bed and decided to call for supper. After a bath she'd get some sleep. They had an early start in the morning and plenty of time to talk during the journey to the mine, she reassured herself, until it occurred to her that she might not be travelling there with Tadj.

CHAPTER ELEVEN

FLYING IN A helicopter was more fun than she'd expected, though it took a moment before Lucy got used to seeing the ground dropping away beneath her feet through the clear bubble. She wasn't frightened with Tadj in control. He was a font of calm—when he wasn't driving her crazy in any number of imaginative ways. As the black aircraft, with its wolf, fangs bared, Tadj's insignia, emblazoned on the side in gold, soared away from the ground at an acute angle, she wondered if she'd ever seen anyone so focused, so sexy and confident, or so utterly and completely in control.

It was just a pity she couldn't read his mind. In the three months they'd been apart, they'd both changed. The man she'd thought such fun, and so dangerously easy to know, had turned out to be the hard-bitten ruler of a powerful country, while she was the woman expecting his child, a fact that had made her more stubbornly determined than ever to do the right thing for her baby, whatever that cost her in personal terms. She did miss the sexy, teasing guy in the coffee shop and couldn't help wondering what life would have been like with him.

'Okay?' Tadj demanded, his voice metallic and impersonal in her headphones.

'Fine,' she fired back.

She reassured herself that his insignia might be a wolf with its fangs bared, but Tadj cared deeply for his country and its people, and even if she were a passing novelty for the Emir of Qalala, and one he might dispense with once their child was born, she believed there was nothing to fear from him. He wasn't evil like her stepfather, a man whose wealth and power had been tainted by the misery he'd caused.

'Are you warmer?' he asked.

Did he care, or was he just being polite? 'I'm very comfortable,' she said honestly. She was looking forward to the adventure ahead.

They didn't speak again until the golden carpet of the desert gave way to a rough dun scrubland. The foothills of the mountains where the mines were located, Lucy guessed. Tadj confirmed this when she asked him if they were getting close.

'I have a project for you,' he added to Lucy's surprise.

'A project?' She followed his gaze through the floor to the rough terrain beneath them, and then flashed a questioning gaze across the flight deck.

'Your final assessment at college just took on a new and exciting slant,' he said, clearly loving the mystery he was causing.

'Did it?' Lucy frowned.

'Combining business with pleasure should be a bonus for you.'

What did that statement mean?

'Your stepfather's activities have prompted me to take certain steps.'

'Really?' Ice shot through Lucy at Tadj's mention of

a man who could inspire terror inside her like no one else. Besides, what more could he do? He'd already arranged for her mother to stay in a safe house and there was no way her stepfather's reach could extend to Qalala, was there?

Tadj's profile was fierce. This was the Warrior King. She could accept that the Emir of Qalala must protect his country, but what was this project he'd mentioned?

'Can I ask about the project?'

Her voice was tinny in his ear. Even so, he heard a quaver. 'Not now.' Preparations for landing took precedence.

Planning ahead was crucial. He was a forward-thinking man whose success drove the revival of Qalala. No one was allowed to disrupt his plans, not even the mother of his unborn child.

'Who are all these people?' Lucy asked with surprise, as the size of the crowd waiting to greet them became apparent.

'My team at the mine and their families,' he explained as he brought the aircraft down in a steady descent. 'Any excuse for a party,' he murmured dryly. His mood took an upturn as he spotted many familiar faces.

'They're very pleased to see you,' Lucy commented as she stared down.

He had brought Lucy here to the sapphire mines in Qalala, not so she could gauge his popularity, but so she could see the scope of his work, and appreciate the heritage their child would one day enjoy. There was no question that his heir, boy or girl, would experience a childhood away from Qalala. He was excited at the prospect of sharing all his desert lore, and introducing his child to their people, and to the glories of his beautiful country. Of course, as his mistress Lucy could be part of that. He wanted to keep her close. On a professional front, she'd be a positive asset, and he was a respecter of talent, who nurtured it wherever he found it. With the best cutters and polishers and jewellery designers working for him, he was keen to encourage new ideas when it came to displaying the jeweller's art. Lucy had recently won a prestigious prize at her college for work on the various exhibitions she'd arranged, making her an ideal candidate for him to draft into the team.

'We'll be staying here for the next few days,' he informed her. 'Roughing it,' he explained, 'so you'll get a chance to know the business—and me,' he added dryly. 'That is what you want, isn't it?'

'Yes,' she admitted, turning to stare at him.

Even allowing for the restrictions of the sound transmission on board, he detected tension in her voice, and by the time the aircraft had settled on its skids, silence was well established between them.

It was exciting to be here. There was a gritty reality about everything surrounding her, and, whatever project Tadj had in mind, she could only take things one step at a time. She had to make the most of this amazing opportunity to tour a sapphire mine with someone who could answer all her questions. That might not be Tadj, but, if nothing else, this trip would add gravitas to her CV. She had travelled to the source of the precious gems and was about to follow that journey through. With her baby's future to think about, there was no better building block for her career.

And her heart? Would have to take a back seat for now. Tadj had talked about roughing it, Lucy remembered, smiling ruefully as she looked around. If this was roughing it, she wasn't the only one who needed to get real. Tadj could certainly do with a reality check. This particular shelter, situated on the fringe of a city of tents, was as well equipped as any hotel. There was even a screened-off area at the back, where she could swim in a rock-shielded part of the lagoon. The biggest natural bathroom in the world, Lucy concluded wryly as she pulled back the hanging dividing tent from lagoon to peer outside.

'Do you like your new quarters?'

Her hand flew to her mouth as Tadj strode into the pavilion. 'Don't you knock?'

He almost smiled. 'Fist on canvas is pretty useless.'

'You gave me a shock,' she admitted, straightening up as she turned to face him.

'Don't slip and fall into the water,' he cautioned.

She could hear music in the distance, and its catchy rhythm only seemed to highlight the tension in the tent. 'There's feasting and dancing tonight,' Tadj explained. 'At the wish of my people, I'll be attending, and I expect you to be there too.'

Expect, she thought. What else did the Emir of Qalala *expect*?

'I'd love to come along,' she said, determined not to be overwhelmed by Tadj's majesty at any point.

He shrugged, stinging her with his careless attitude. She ached inside, missing the friendship that had sprung up so easily between them on that first night. She missed the camaraderie and banter they'd shared, but had no intention of grovelling to try to reclaim Tadj's favour. He might be like a mountain, towering and inflexible, but he had to move too.

'I'll bathe first,' she said, glancing in the direction of

the lagoon. The chance to refresh her mind as well as her body was well overdue.

'I'll bathe with you,' Tadj informed her. 'You should have someone with you when you swim.'

'I'm a strong swimmer,' Lucy protested as her pulse began to race off the scale.

'And pregnant,' Tadj said flatly. 'All open water holds risks.'

So much for solitude and time to think, but why antagonise him? She could shrug too, and, turning her back, she stripped down to her underwear. One good thing about growing up in gangland luxury was the unlimited use of a heated indoor pool at home, as well as a tennis court, and access to a string of ponies. When Lucy's father had been alive, the same property had been a simple hill farm where Lucy's parents had scratched a living. But they'd been such happy, uncomplicated times. When her father had died all that had changed. Lucy's mother had thought it a dream come true when a handsome stranger had whisked her off her feet, but that fairy tale had soon turned into a nightmare, and the simple hill farm had been transformed into a fortress, guarded by grim-faced men with automatic weapons.

'Lucy?'

The sharp note in Tadj's voice jolted her back to the present. Crossing her arms over her chest, as if he didn't know every inch of her body already, she glanced at him, wishing things could be different. Shielded by the tent, and by the towering mountain behind it, she had thought about swimming naked, but having Tadj join her in the black boxers he'd stripped down to was danger enough. She gasped when he put an arm around her waist. 'Sharps rocks,' he warned. 'Lean on me.'

The water was frigid with ice-melt from the mountains, but as they swam alongside each other Tadj steered her towards the cliff face where a waterfall was crashing down. *What?* She turned to look at him midstroke. If this was his idea of safety, she didn't think much of it. She should have known he'd guide her through to the other side of the pounding cascade where they were completely shielded from the outside world. Holding her in place with his hard, wet body pinning her against the smooth rock, he remarked, 'You swim well.'

Resting his forearms above her head, he made sure she wasn't going anywhere. 'And so do you,' she conceded, staring at him levelly.

She wanted this more than anything, and yet dreaded the moment when Tadj broke down the emotional barriers dividing them, because that meant laying her heart on the line for the Emir of Qalala to trample. Tadj lost no time in claiming his reward. As the freezing torrent thundered around them, he drove his mouth down on hers.

Tadj was a madness she could never refuse—never wanted to lose—and she responded with matching passion. He was as vital to her existence as air to breathe, food to eat, and the heat of his body, together with the chill of the icy water, created a force that went way beyond caution. Upping the stakes, she wrapped her legs around his waist. She gasped, knowing she would never get used to the passion between them. This might not be how she'd planned the immediate future to pan out, but if sex was all they had...

Tadj soon removed her bra and thong, and it was his turn to groan with pleasure as he mapped her naked body. 'Yes!' he hissed between his teeth, taking her firmly with one smooth thrust of his hips. From there it was a crazy race to the finish, while she worked with him, matching his force. They couldn't get enough of each other, so no sooner was one violent release achieved, than they were pursuing the next. Some wild force had possessed them, and as Tadj raked his sharp black stubble against her neck, she bit his shoulder, urging him on with words she barely recognised. They were like two animals in the prime of life, mating fiercely and unaware of anything else.

'*Yes!*' she screamed, not even trying to hold back when each shattering release had her in its grip. Sometimes sensation could be enough, and this was one of those times. Tadj had always been the consummate lover, and even here in the lagoon, with water crashing around them, he made sure that he extracted every available pulse of pleasure, and when she was quiet again, he teased her into awareness, by moving steadily and carefully, until her weary little bud had sparked back to life again.

'Oh, yes,' Lucy crooned as Tadj maintained a dependable and steady rhythm. Nestling her head against his chest, she let him do all the work, while she rested, floating in the water, concentrating on the place that had become the centre of her universe. He knew just what to do, how to stimulate and encourage, and it wasn't long before she was on the edge again.

'Now,' he instructed in a whisper against her ear.

'Oh, yes,' she groaned thankfully, as he pushed her over the edge into pleasure with a few firm thrusts.

'Once more, I think,' he said when she rested, gasping for breath.

'No, I'm done,' she said groggily, glad of his hands supporting her buttocks as she hung replete in his arms.

'I don't think so,' Tadj argued. 'I know you, and there's more. Shall I prove it to you?'

'Please,' she begged, loving the way his big hands tightened on her buttocks.

'You don't have to do anything, except experience pleasure,' he murmured in a low, husky tone.

How many lovers had used these cooling waters to sate their heated passion? She and Tadj were part of the lagoon's history now. That was Lucy's last thought before pleasure invaded her mind, and, for now, pleasure was enough.

They left the lagoon swimming side by side with long, leisurely strokes. Lucy's limbs felt heavy, and she felt sated. It was almost as if neither of them was in a hurry to return to dry land, where reality ruled. That sense of reality was challenged as soon as she climbed out of the water and spotted a pile of fresh towels left ready for them on the bank. This wasn't her usual reality, Lucy concluded as she wrapped a towel around her body, and the towels only emphasised the point that the Emir of Qalala was never completely alone; nor would his private life remain private for long.

But whatever else happened today, she had this to remember, she thought as Tadj secured a towel around his washboard waist.

Back in the tent, Lucy was surprised to find a silk tunic with matching silk trousers, in a soft shade of cerulean blue, waiting for her on the bed. It was the same style she'd noticed the Qalalan women wearing. Their fashions had intrigued her, as they were more active wear than purely decorative.

'Do you like them?' Tadj asked. 'It's a perfect outfit for the party,' he said, skimming a glance over the outfit.

'The party?' Lucy queried. 'I thought we'd get chance to talk. After all, we've got a lot to sort out…'

Tadj's stare was cool. He'd switched to Emir in an instant. Well, if he thought she was a candidate for his harem, he could think again.

'If my people organise a party to welcome me back, that takes precedence over everything else.'

Gritting her teeth, she reminded herself not to lose her cool. This was Tadj's kingdom, and she was his guest. 'Of course. I'll be proud to be your guest.'

'You'll be attending as my mistress,' Tadj rapped out.

'Do you intend to make an official announcement to that effect?' Lucy exclaimed with frustration. She'd never tacitly agreed that she would become his mistress. In fact she'd hoped he wouldn't hold her to that now everything about her stepfather was out in the open and he'd already put plans into place to deal with him.

Besides, she didn't fit the brief of any man's mistress, especially not the Emir of Qalala's. She was far too independent to be locked away in a fort awaiting His Majesty's pleasure—not to mention the fact that she'd been spared the flamboyant good looks she imagined must be necessary to hold down the post of official mistress. She didn't possess the sophistication, or the class to mix in high society. She was happiest with her friends at the laundry, or with her student chums at college, where she dressed as they did, in cheap tops and jeans. Above and beyond all that, she was about to become a mother, and with a child to support, as well as a career to plan, she didn't have time to waste swanning about.

'I won't need to announce anything,' Tadj informed her with a relaxed shrug, with about as much emotion as if they'd been discussing the weather. 'And, rest assured, I've no intention of embarrassing you.'

'Your people will guess when they see me at your side?' Lucy supposed.

'Correct,' he agreed.

CHAPTER TWELVE

'AS WE'VE DISCUSSED, arrangements have been made to keep your mother safe.'

'Thank you.'

'However,' he continued, brushing off her gratitude, 'until I receive certain reassurances, you will stay in Qalala.' Tadj's stare was penetrating. 'I understand that you had to get away, and would do anything—use anyone—to make sure that happened.'

'Please don't look at me like that. I never set out to get pregnant, but I'm glad that I am.'

'Can I believe you?'

'You must,' she insisted softly.

'For the sake of our child?' Tadj suggested. 'I suppose I'll never know what you were thinking three months ago. I can only make plans going forward from now.'

Anger surged inside her. They were both in the wrong, and she had no intention of being painted as the only sinner. 'How do you think I feel, when you ask me to be your mistress, to satisfy your sexual urges?'

'*My* sexual urges?' Tadj laughed out loud. 'That's rich, coming from you. Bottom line,' he snapped, before Lucy had chance to speak, 'you're under my protection, and there you will stay—and that includes you, your mother, and the baby.'

'Our baby,' she fired back. 'And my stepfather? What are you going to do about him? No one's safe while he's roaming free.'

'Your stepfather has been returned to jail where he belongs, and he won't be coming out of prison ever again, once my investigators have shared their information.'

Lucy was stunned into silence. She couldn't believe that her stepfather's tyranny was at an end. It meant she was free, and her mother was safe. Tadj had accomplished the seemingly impossible, by lifting a lifetime of fear and dread from her shoulders. 'It's really over?' she whispered as she marvelled at this fact.

'And always will be from now on,' Tadj confirmed. 'I wish you'd told me from the start.'

'We hardly knew each other,' she pointed out. 'I wouldn't burden you with that on the first day we met.'

'All the same, I wish you had,' Tadj told her.

'How can I ever thank you?' she asked.

'I'll think of something,' he promised with one of his dark, unreadable looks. 'But now you'd better get ready for the party. That's one way you can repay me tonight.'

By keeping up a good front, Lucy thought, longing for more as Tadj added, 'Call your mother. Let her know the good news, and then get ready. I'll return to collect you in half an hour.'

'Half an hour,' Lucy agreed tensely, knowing the phone call would take up every moment of that time.

What Lucy could never have expected was that several women would approach the tent just as she had tearfully ended the call to her mother and offer to help Lucy get

ready for the party. It was impossible not to succumb to
their warmth and friendliness. The way they had welcomed her to their community reminded Lucy of her
first day at the laundry, where she'd made so many new
friends. Just like them, these women were full of ad-
vice on how to wear her hair, and what make-up to put
on. Language wasn't a barrier as several of them spoke
English fluently.

'You should grow your hair,' one of the women insisted, and when Lucy asked why, she was told that a
lover liked to run his fingers through long hair, while
another, bolder woman, suggested other uses, when it
came to teasing a man into a state where he would agree
to anything. Lucy laughed with them, and said that her
hair would have to do, and that whatever help they gave
her, she would never be glamorous as they were. In Lucy's opinion, their exotic sloe-eyed beauty completely
eclipsed her own Celtic complexion with its peppering
of freckles. This statement was greeted by a chorus of
disagreement, but what would Tadj think? she wondered
when one of the women had directed her to a full-length
mirror. Gone was the utilitarian outfit she had arrived in,
and in its place was a two-piece of such exquisite work-
manship she felt like a queen.

Queen for a night, Lucy reflected ruefully as the
women tweaked and smoothed the delicate fabric of her
trousers and matching tunic. There wasn't much they
could do with her short haircut other than to place a single hibiscus blossom behind her ear.

So, hang me, I'm excited, she thought, imagining
Tadj's expression when he saw her all dressed up for the
party. Even after everything that had happened between
them, the prospect of spending time with the sometimes

forbidding Emir of Qalala made her face burn and her body sing hallelujah in four-part harmony.

'You look beautiful,' one of the older woman told her. 'The Emir won't be able to resist you.'

'He'll fall in love with you,' another insisted.

Lucy's shoulders slumped. Somehow, she doubted that.

'You're ready, I see.'

She whirled around to find Tadj standing behind her. He was silhouetted in the opening of the tent, backed by the blaze of countless campfires, and the sight of him dressed in traditional desert garb was enough to convince her that Lucy Gillingham was indeed a lost cause. Her pulse was racing, while her body was going crazy in the presence of her all-powerful fantasy desert Sheikh made all too heart-stoppingly real. In a simple black tunic, with loose-fitting trousers and a headdress wrapped around his fiercely handsome face, this desert king was sex on two hard-muscled legs. She was smitten all over again.

Love swelled inside her. As did doubt. The power of his presence was undeniably formidable, but did Tadj respect her as the mother of his child, or was she a convenient womb, to be dismissed as soon as their baby was safely delivered? For a woman who had seized control of her life and had been steering it in a steady and constant direction for some time now, it was unnerving to know that this was one situation over which she had no control.

Lucy's stepfather had been a problem, which Tadj had dealt with in his usual incisive way. She wouldn't be troubled again. Even after everything they'd been through, he wouldn't change a thing, Tadj concluded as he stared past the group of smiling women to the only woman who could turn his life upside down. Lucy looked stunning tonight, though he'd put her on show, and had expected her to behave a certain way, and that while she was vulnerable and her life was under the microscope. To her credit, she hadn't let him down. It remained to be seen how she would handle tonight's raw desert gathering.

Lucy proved to have a natural friendly way with everyone. How could he have forgotten that? he wondered, remembering her many friends at the laundry as he took in the crowd that had gathered around her on cushions in front of the open fire. With one of the older women acting as Lucy's unofficial interpreter, he wondered if the questions would ever end, though she fielded all of them with grace and humour, which was more than he deserved.

She felt his gaze on her, and stared at him in a way that made him want to join her immediately, but it was time for him to receive the fealty of the heads of tribes. He felt her continuing interest as he did this, and briefly wished he could offer Lucy more, but, until the law of the land was changed, Qalala expected him to make a politically advantageous marriage, and to please his people that would have to be soon.

When the formalities were over, he stripped off his top. Lucy seemed surprised when he dumped it onto the cushion next to her.

'Are we about to give a practical demonstration of my place in your world?' she asked discreetly.

Her words made him instantly hard, but he shot her a look, to warn her not to try his patience. No one addressed the Emir of Qalala in front of his people in a disrespectful way. 'I am preparing for the games,' he informed her.

Pulling her head back, she gave him one of her looks. 'Didn't I just say that?'

'The desert games,' he said patiently, though a betraying twitch of his lips might have given him away. No one could make him laugh at himself like Lucy.

'Indeed,' she said, flinching when someone handed him a sabre. 'Don't cut yourself with that.'

'I'll try not to,' he assured her. Dipping at the waist, he brought his mouth close to her ear. 'Rest assured, no one has lost their life at one of these gatherings yet.'

'There's always a first time,' she said brightly.

His warning look was completely wasted, though she did have the good grace to look alarmed when one of the tribesmen brought up his horse.

'Is that thing even safe to ride?'

With a brief ironic glance, he leapt onto the back of his black stallion. 'We shall see,' he murmured.

'Just remember,' she said, springing up and grabbing the bridle, 'you've got responsibilities now.'

'You're beginning to sound like a wife,' he commented as he wheeled his horse around.

'And you're the very spit of a delinquent husband,' she yelled after him as he galloped away.

He should be angry, but he wanted Lucy too much to be impatient with her for long, and, with the heat of competition on him, he was keen to get these games over with, and turn lust into reality. Whatever the outcome, Lucy would be in his bed tonight, where he'd be sure to make her pay, and in the most pleasurable way imaginable, for her unadulterated cheek.

Stay safe, you stubborn son-of-a-she-wolf, Lucy thought, clenching her fists with anxiety as she watched Tadj line up with the other riders, all of whom were mounted on spirited horses. There were women in the mix, she noticed with interest. So why was she sitting by the fireside? She was a damn good rider, and had been happy on horseback since her father had strapped her into a basket saddle on an old Shetland pony when she could barely walk. And these desert games weren't so much violent as skilful, she decided as a huge cheer went up. Riders raced down a torchlit track in pairs towards a gourd hanging from a pole. That was exactly the type of game she'd played with her friends. The first jockey to cut the gourd and return to the start line was the winner. Her gaze flashed to the pony lines, where several likely-looking animals stood waiting...

What the hell was she doing? Tadj's pulse rocketed as he spotted Lucy vaulting onto the back of a half-wild Arab pony. He yelled a warning, but, leaning low over the animal's neck as it broke into a flat-out gallop, she couldn't hear him.

And she accused him of taking risks!

Quitting the race, he wheeled his horse around and chased after her. The track was long and full of riders; so many that the youths whose job it was to hang the gourds could hardly keep up. Just as he reached her, Lucy seized a gourd, spun her pony around, and flashed past him. Brandishing the prize high in triumph provoked ear-splitting cheers from the crowd. She might be a stranger in their midst, but she was their champion tonight, and her surprise win had made her the spectators' favourite. Not his, he thought grimly as he urged his horse to catch up with hers. Seizing Lucy around the waist, he lifted her onto his galloping stallion, which provoked another round of cheers. Not surprisingly, Lucy was distinctly unimpressed.

'What the hell do you think you're doing?' she yelled at him in fury.

'Saving you from yourself,' he retorted grimly as he tightened his grip. Taking her back at a steady canter to the pony lines, he dismounted and carefully lifted her down.

'I don't know what you think you're playing at,' she said, throwing him off. 'I knew what I was doing. That was just an advanced version of the games we used to play when I was a child on the farm.'

'And were you pregnant at that time?' he remarked coolly.

'Don't you dare suggest I'd take risks with my baby,' she warned as he led her away.

'Well, you're not playing games on my watch,' he said, adding, 'especially not dangerous games,' as he escorted her back to her tent.

'Why not? Aren't rowdy games an appropriate pastime for your mistress?' Before he could answer, she added hotly, 'There were plenty of other women taking part—as well as children.'

'My interest is you—and *you*, in case you had forgotten, are pregnant.'

'Really? I'm your only interest? You could have fooled me,' she snapped. 'You ignore me most of the time, unless a particular type of carnal hunger strikes you, of course.'

'Which it never does for you,' he fired back, realising as he did so that, while no one could make him laugh like Lucy, no one could rouse every one of his carefully contained emotions as she could. He had never felt this heated before. Lucy's safety, and that of their child, were paramount.

'So, is it because I'm a woman that you object to my riding in the games, or because I'm your woman?'

'Because you're pregnant!' he roared, seemingly unable to get his point across.

'So now you care?' she mocked.

Pregnancy hormones, he thought as her eyes welled with tears. Upbeat one minute, she was on the edge of an emotional meltdown the next. He'd been doing some reading, as well as investigating, since Lucy had catapulted back into his life, and recognised the signs. 'Of course I care,' he insisted, then realised he was shouting. He never lost control—*ever*. Consumed by frustration, he snatched the sabre out of her hands, and tossed it to a waiting attendant.

'I'm pregnant, not sick,' she insisted as he ushered her inside the tent.

'You're a damn nuisance,' he spat out. 'What if you'd been hurt?'

'You could send me back as damaged goods,' she flashed, her eyes welling again, 'and recruit a new mistress.'

'Now you're being ridiculous,' he insisted with an impatient gesture.

'Am I?' she flared. 'You bring me here with one thing in mind, which is to be your official mistress. Knowing I wouldn't agree, you trump up excuses about some job or other—anything to get me here.'

'Which should tell you how much I care.'

'It tells me you're a complete control freak.'

'And what about you?' he argued. 'Deceit got you here, and has carried you through this far. Am I supposed to think better of you now?'

'I don't care what you think,' she railed, her voice shaking. 'I did what I had to.'

'You do care.' Grabbing her arms, he held her still.

'You care too much, which is why you're always trying to please everyone.'

'And failing miserably, I suppose.'

He couldn't bear to see Lucy hugging herself defensively. 'Yes,' he confirmed. The truth might be harsh, but it was preferable to how they'd handled things so far.

'All right,' she said. Straightening up, she lowered her arms. 'I will stay, but only on mutually acceptable terms.'

He dipped his head to stare into her eyes. 'You're setting terms now?'

'You bet I am,' she told him. 'What's so funny?' she asked. 'Just because you're not used to people standing up to you, doesn't mean I'm willing to fall in line. I need to work to support myself and the baby, but I'm extremely keen to learn as much as I can about our child's heritage, which is why I want to stay on in Qalala—at least while I'm on holiday from college.'

'So, being with me has nothing to do with your decision?'

Frowning deeply, she remained silent.

Shaking his head slowly, he stared into Lucy's fierce and determined eyes. She was as stubborn as he was. 'You are, without doubt, the most annoying woman I have ever met.'

'I would hate to come second,' she said.

'No chance of that.' Nudging her inside the tent, he dismissed their attendants. 'Sit,' he instructed.

'Sit yourself—or am I to be lectured like a child?'

Anything but a child, Lucy was a beautiful woman, who was carrying his baby, and he could think of no better mother. How to cope with Lucy's spirit was a question for another day, but did he want to clip her wings? Could he offer her enough to make it worth her while to stay?

Money didn't interest her, so for once in his charmed life he wasn't sure. 'As I mentioned on the flight here, I have a proposition for you—and it's something that doesn't hang on you becoming my mistress.'

'Well, that's a relief,' she said.

'Allow me to pause while I take in your compliment.'

'So, what is it?' she said, green eyes narrowing with suspicion.

'I'm offering you a job as part of my team in the sapphire division. You'd be paid the same as everyone else. Anything else is up to you.'

'And, what would the job entail?'

'Designing an exhibition for the best of the jewellery. I want to create a heritage museum here on site, as well as a touring exhibition.'

'Quite a small job, then,' she said dryly, but there was a distinct glint of interest in her eyes.

'Quite insignificant,' he agreed, acting stern.

'I'd be a tiny cog in a huge wheel,' she said thoughtfully.

'Correct. But each cog has something unique to offer, and, without it, the smooth running of the machine cannot be guaranteed.'

'You put it so persuasively,' she observed dryly.

'That was my intention,' he confessed with the hint of a smile.

'Are you serious?' she asked. 'I mean, this is like my dream job.'

'Never more so. Why waste your education?'

'If I agree, you can't treat me as if I'm made of glass.'

'I won't hesitate to pass an opinion,' he warned.

'And neither will I,' she countered with spirit.

'I would expect nothing less of you.' And, done with talking, he brought her into his arms.

'You've got a cheek.'

'Yes,' he murmured. 'And you have a beautiful body.'

'When can I see the mine and the museum?'

'When I say you can.'

'And when will that be?'

'You have to earn the privilege.'

As he held her still, she softened. 'When can I begin?' she asked, searching his eyes in a way that made him instantly hard.

'Right now?'

They only had to look into each other's eyes for understanding to spring between them. They were so well matched, and Lucy could always surprise him, he thought as she sank to her knees in front of him, not to bow in gratitude—oh, no, she'd never do that—but to wrap her mouth around him over the fine linen of his trousers until he couldn't think straight.

'Who's in control now?' she lifted her head to whisper.

Throwing his head back, he laughed, but shocked pleasure soon silenced him as she tightened her mouth around. Waves of sensation punched through him, and he groaned involuntarily as he opened his mouth to drag in some much-needed air. And this wasn't all she had in mind. Her nimble fingers were soon working on the fastening at his waist, and she freed him in no time.

The heat of Lucy's mouth on his engorged flesh was indescribable. Sufficient to say that the rasp of her tongue promised release like never before.

CHAPTER THIRTEEN

'YOU NEED THIS…we both do…'

'Witch,' he groaned as Lucy took control.

'Just to warn you, I'm no man's mistress,' she said as he laced his fingers through her hair to keep her close. 'I'm doing this because I want to.'

'Don't I know it,' he grated out.

Lucy's husky tone betrayed her arousal, but this was on her terms, and the challenge she gave him never failed to arouse.

She carried out her threat with surprising skill, but when he remarked on this, she said, 'I think I should know what you like by now.'

With a bellow of agony, he lifted her and dispensed with her clothes. Settling her onto him, he proved her right about them both needing this. Working furiously towards the inevitable conclusion, they brought each other to the edge efficiently, and within a few firm strokes they were plunged into pleasure so extreme it left them sated, and yet hungry for more.

'Not tonight,' Lucy said matter-of-factly. Sweeping up her clothes, she added, 'I'll give you my decision about the job tomorrow, after I've visited the sapphire mines, which will obviously impact on my decision to stay—so you'll get that too.'

'That's a lot of giving,' he commented as they locked eyes. 'Give yourself first,' he advised. 'You'll enjoy it, and it will help you sleep.'

She looked at him as if she couldn't quite believe he could match her for detachment. Whatever it took, he thought as they stared at each other.

Breath rushed from her lungs as he swung her into his arms, and she yelped when he dropped her on the bed. 'You're a very bad man,' she remarked with an expression that teased and tormented him.

'That I am,' he agreed. To pretend otherwise would mean a sleepless night for both of them, and what was the point in that?

Tadj was the most amazing lover. He made every part of her body sing, and he was right about her not being able to resist him. Why should she, when all she had to do was close her eyes and concentrate on pleasure? His steady breathing countering her hectic gasps made her all the more excited, and the crashing release that followed rocked her body and soul. She couldn't chart the moment when extreme pleasure turned to exhaustion, and finally sleep, but when she woke in Tadj's arms in the morning, it was the happiest moment of her life.

'I love you,' she whispered, safe in the knowledge that he was still fast asleep.

He grunted faintly, but didn't stir, which was a relief, because laying her heart bare put her entirely at Tadj's mercy. Tuned to her every mood, he wasn't long in waking. She was lying on her side with her back to him, which meant that Tadj only had to make the smallest adjustment to his position to take her from behind.

Arching her back, she raised her hips to make herself even more available for pleasure. Lazy lovemaking like this was the perfect way to start a day. Clutching a pillow, she concentrated on sensations, and nothing else.

'Better?' Tadj soothed when she tumbled noisily off the cliff edge. Moving convulsively to claim the last pulse of pleasure, she was incapable of speech. 'Is that what you needed?' he crooned huskily, with a smile of very masculine triumph in his tone.

She could only groan with contentment when he started again. 'See what happens when you're a very good girl,' he murmured.

'I can't be good all the time,' she warned.

'I noticed,' he said, seeming pleased.

'And I'm no pushover,' she insisted groggily, with a small contented smile.

'Of course not,' Tadj confirmed.

'Did I detect a faint mocking note in your voice?' she challenged, turning her head to spear a stare into his eyes.

'Did I detect some residual need here?' he countered, teasing her in the way she loved.

To hell with it! Thrusting her hips, she claimed him.

What a wonderful day, Lucy thought, feeling elated as she pulled on her jeans and top after bathing in the lagoon. Her body was still tingling from Tadj's expert lovemaking. She wanted more. She would always want more, where Tadj was concerned, though she was excited to see what came next when they visited the sapphire mines.

First, there was a short journey by helicopter, which Tadj piloted once again, and when they landed, he announced, 'We'll take the SUV from here.'

His excitement was infectious. Gone was the stern and

aloof Emir, and in his place *at last* was the guy she'd met in a café. 'Are you up for it?' he asked, nuzzling her neck.

'For everything,' she said, sharing a scorching look.

He was so hot, how was she ever going to concentrate? Lucy wondered as they climbed into the vehicle. Tadj's profile was all the more appealing for being so stern. He made her want his arms around her. With forearms like steel girders, deeply tanned and dusted with just the right amount of jet-black hair, there was no surprise there. Tadj was a stunning sight, in bed or out of it—but more complex than she had ever imagined.

'Some seams of sapphire are found in rock and call for conventional mining methods,' he explained in the low, husky tone that made her body thrill with pleasure. He glanced across, the heat in his gaze suggesting Tadj knew that Lucy's focus wasn't solely on the precious gems. 'Others turn up in streams, or even in the silt of a *wadi*, and need nothing more than a sieve to fish them out. What?' he asked.

'You,' Lucy admitted. 'I like you better up here in the mountains. You're a different man.'

'Than the one who was in bed with you a couple of hours ago?' His mocking frown teased every part of her as he leaned across to drop a kiss on her neck. 'I'm the same man with different interests,' he said, straightening up again.

What did the future hold? she wondered. It was all too easy to think that Tadj, in his banged-up jeans and a simple black top, really was the fun guy she'd met in a café, and it was tough remembering he was the Emir of Qalala, with a different life from hers.

The trip to the mine brightened things up again. It went much better than Lucy had hoped. She was fascinated by the work underground, where the air was warm and still, and on the ground where the mountain breezes whipped at her clothes as she watched the sapphires go through their initial sorting. Tadj had an enthusiastic team in place, and the very latest in equipment, and she couldn't help but want to be part of it, to the point where she was already working on some ideas for the exhibition.

'I think we could improve things here at your heritage centre,' she told Tadj frankly, when he invited comments from the team. 'You have some of the world's most spectacular jewels on display in what appears to me to be an uninviting warehouse. Visitors should be taken on a journey—a pictorial tour of all the various mining methods, where they can see examples of rough stones before they're cut, and then the polished jewels, both before and after they're set.'

As murmurs of agreement rose from his team, he knew he'd made the right choice in Lucy. Whether that was enough to persuade her to stay in Qalala was the big question, and remained to be seen.

'There needs to be a lush floor covering that creates a hushed atmosphere of wonder and awe,' she went on. 'And, of course, discreet lighting—and music to set the mood.'

'I can see your enthusiasm is infectious,' he told her as they left to smiling goodbyes, leaving his team to discuss the latest ideas.

His staff had arranged a picnic by the *wadi* where he and Lucy could spend time alone. It had rained recently, so the dried-up riverbed now provided a perfect swimming pool, where they could freshen up and cool down after a busy morning touring the mine. As the blistering heat of late afternoon slipped into the cooler lilac light of dusk they settled down to enjoy the feast his chefs had prepared, which was both simple and delicious, made even more so by freshly squeezed juice that his attendants had thoughtfully left cool in bottles they'd tethered in the stream.

Rolling onto his back, he stared up at the bowl of sky overhead, as it turned from a clear, cloudless blue to gold and crimson, as the day moved slowly into night. A chill breeze blew up as the lavender dusk, threaded through with smoky grey, lost its colour completely as the sun disappeared behind the mountains.

'This is even more beautiful than anything I've seen so far,' Lucy enthused softly at his side. 'You live in the most ravishing country. I'm not sure you deserve it,' she added, turning onto her stomach to stare at him with a cheeky sideways frown.

He laughed as he drew her into his arms. He was a man as well as an emir, but when he kissed Lucy Gillingham he felt like the king of the world. Seeing everything through Lucy's eyes had given him the greatest pleasure imaginable today. And she was right in that Qalala was beautiful. He found it even more so with Lucy at his side. 'So, you'll stay?' he whispered, feeling confident he knew her answer.

'For a fixed contract,' she agreed. 'I think that would be sensible, don't you?'

What he thought wasn't printable. Pulling back, he stared at her. That certainly wasn't the answer he'd expected. 'The jewellery you've seen must tour the world in the New Year, which means that time is at a premium.'

'It can't be organised exclusively to your timetable. I have a baby to consider.'

Anger and frustration propelled him up. Why was it that nothing was ever certain with Lucy?

'I have college to finish,' she reminded him as she clambered to her feet. 'I need my qualifications before I have the baby.'

'I have forgotten nothing,' he assured her coolly. 'And, as you have just so eloquently pointed out, the clock is ticking.'

'I'm going home for Christmas,' she informed him.

'Home?' he queried.

'Yes. Back to the laundry.'

'And if that doesn't suit me?'

'Look,' she said, obviously trying to be reasonable. 'I don't want to appear ungrateful for the wonderful offer you've made me here, or spoil what has been a memorable and very special day. I'm longing to work with your team. In fact, I feel quite passionately about it, as if it were meant to be.'

'But you're not passionate about staying with me?'

'I didn't say that. And it isn't true. It's just that some things are sacrosanct to me, and standing on my own feet is one of those things.'

'Even now when you've seen all this?' he said, spreading his arms wide to encompass everything he could offer. It wasn't just a job. He wanted Lucy to stay with him. And, yes, as his mistress to begin with, but things could always change. Like any other country, Qalala needed time to adjust, and in the meantime Lucy would have every privilege he could provide.

'Let me stop you there,' she said when he began to explain. 'I understand that a man like you can probably do anything he pleases, but that first you have to make sure your people are safe and Qalala's boundaries are strong.

I accept that those boundaries can be extended to Qalala's advantage through marriage—which is exactly why I must plough my own furrow.'

'I care for you more than you know,' he said fiercely.

'Then, let me go,' Lucy said, her eyes welling with tears.

'I can't,' he admitted grimly. 'I want you and I want our child, *here* in Qalala.'

'But when it comes to your duty, you can't. Tadj, there is no easy way.'

'No quick way, certainly,' he agreed.

He could offer Lucy nothing at this precise moment, and he would not raise her hopes with empty promises. 'Whatever you decide,' he rapped out.

Now it came to losing her, reality had struck home forcibly, so that each word he uttered to ease her journey home was like a dagger in his heart.

'You will both be well provided for,' he added in a clipped tone to hide how that made him feel.

Lucy actually flinched as if he'd hit her. 'You're buying me off,' she said.

'I will do my duty by you,' he confirmed stiffly.

'If you can't see how that hurts me, I think we're both right; I must go. There's nothing left to say,' she added. 'But no money. I've never been interested in your material wealth. It's you I care about,' she admitted. 'And you care about Qalala, which is how it should be. We're both bound by promises we've made: you to your country, and me to myself. I don't want half a life like my mother endured, always hoping things will be better. I want to seize life and work hard to provide for my baby. Qalala wouldn't want half your attention, and neither do I. But I do worry about you.'

'You worry about me?' he queried sceptically.

'Yes. If you can't find a way to combine your personal hopes and dreams with what's best for Qalala, I worry that you'll never be happy. And I don't want to make things worse for you, by pulling you this way and that. Nor do I want our baby to grow up with parents at war. It's better that we live apart, and can be happy when we're with our child, than we live together and make each other miserable.'

He took a long time to answer, and then he said coolly, 'That decision is up to you. I would never keep you here against your will.'

'No,' Lucy argued gently, 'that's up to both of us. Because I know you can't change, I'm going to keep to my timetable, and go home as I said I would. I had imagined that when we'd toured the mine, we'd talk and plan for our baby, but you're not ready to do that yet, and maybe you never will be.'

'The sapphire mines bring prosperity to my people, and I won't apologise for focusing on them, because you need to understand what a vital part they play in Qalala's future. You could help with that. You say you want to understand this part of your child's heritage, so stay, and try to accept that my duty to Qalala and its people will always come before my own selfish personal desires.'

'But if you're not happy, how can your people be happy?' Lucy argued with her usual sound common sense. 'And where does our child fit into your master plan? A child changes everything.'

'Do you think I don't know that?'

'Changes everything for both of us, I mean,' she said.

He wasn't used to being lectured and he turned away. 'I suppose you expect me to take you home?' he declared when he was calmer.

'Back to King's Dock?' Lucy queried. 'I'm pretty sure I can find my own way back. I'm equally sure that my going home will be better for both of us. I'll send you my proposal for the exhibition as soon as I've got something to show you. And then, if you're agreeable, I'll take part in meetings online with the team. I don't see a problem handling things that way going forward.'

She was alone in that.

'And when it comes to putting my plans into practice,' she added, 'I'll happily travel anywhere necessary to make sure the team doesn't encounter any snags along the way.'

'With your baby strapped to your back?' he queried tensely.

'If I have to.'

'This is *our* child you're talking about. The child whose upbringing I will take full part in.'

Apprehension flashed across Lucy's face, but she rallied fast to add, 'Then, we'd better make time to talk. As you said, the clock is ticking.'

'I'm sure you've got it all worked out,' he commented bitterly.

'Don't be angry,' she begged. 'I want you to know how much I appreciate this opportunity—'

'Stop! Stop right now,' he insisted. He was done with the emotional battering. 'Make this project part of your final assessment at college.'

'I will,' she said, latching onto his cool tone with what he thought might even be relief.

They really wrung it out of each other, he thought as they stared unblinking into each other's eyes. The bond between them was as tight as ever, and would remain so when their child was born, but when it came to the most

basic human feelings they were both hopeless commu-
nicators.

'I'll miss you,' Lucy said in a wry, offhand way, but
her eyes were sad.

'You don't have to go home right away.'

'I do,' she insisted. 'I've got your brief for the exhibition safe in my head, and we'll keep in touch. We can
talk online and make arrangements when my due date
is closer.'

To discuss the future of their child via a screen over
the internet reminded him of a child sitting on a suitcase,
split between countries and two sets of people, one with
generous hearts, who had wanted him to join them out of
love they weren't afraid to show, while the others' social
lives were more important. His worst nightmare was to
be that type of parent. 'I'll be in touch regularly,' he said.

'Better that we get on with our lives,' Lucy told him.

Raising barriers so neither of them could see the future
was as much his fault as hers, he supposed. His loathing
for her stepfather and the damage that man had done to
Lucy quadrupled as she turned away to hide her tears.
Once hurt, never mended, he thought as they faced up
to the long journey home.

CHAPTER FOURTEEN

LEAVING QALALA WAS AGONY. Leaving on a commercial flight, which Lucy had insisted on taking, only made things worse, because she had to hide her emotions and pretend her heart wasn't breaking. That shouldn't have been too hard for someone who had learned to guard her feelings growing up, but it was, because she might be as buttoned up as Tadj, but surely they should have been able to talk and make plans for their baby? Wasn't that more important than visits to a mine, and schemes for an exhibition?

They were both at fault, Lucy concluded. Tadj was duty-bound to Qalala, and refused to grant himself a private life, while she was equally inflexible when it came to remaining independent. Imagining Tadj marrying for the good of his country tore her up inside. It would destroy him, as well as his wife and any children they might have. Was that the reward of duty? If so, duty was a vindictive mistress, and it was up to Tadj to change things in Qalala. She couldn't help with that, and must concentrate on moving forward to build a stable base for her child. If Tadj wanted to be involved in their baby's upbringing, then so much the better, she would never stop him, but could she afford to put things on hold in the hope that he might?

As the aircraft soared high above the cloud line, she was sad for the things he'd miss. She wanted to share the first precious flutters of life with him, so he could feel the joy she felt at that moment. Maybe he'd had enough of her, and was glad to see her go. He hadn't exactly helped her to pack, but once they'd returned to the fort he'd done everything possible to smooth her journey home. On the one hand, she'd been relieved, because there'd been no ugly scenes between them, but right up to the last minute she'd hoped he'd ask her to stay, so they could somehow work this out.

That was a fantasy too far, Lucy accepted with a sigh as she stared unseeing out of the small window at her side. Tadj's position as the Emir of Qalala would always stop him following his heart. 'I'll get back to you,' he'd said at the airport, where they'd both held in their feelings, parting with a dispassionate kiss on both cheeks.

'About the job?' she'd pressed.

'About everything,' he'd said, and then he'd turned and strode away with a phalanx of royal guards surrounding him, keeping everyone, including Lucy, at bay. That was Tadj's life, his lonely life.

They'd have contact through their joint involvement in the Qalalan sapphire project, if nothing else, Lucy tried to reassure herself, and meanwhile she must concentrate on completing her studies and holding down her jobs. If Tadj delegated his side of the arrangements for their child to a member of staff, it would really hurt, but she'd have to get over that too. In this mood of absolute determination, she pulled out her sketch pad and started work on her initial design for the inaugural exhibition of the world-famous Qalalan sapphires.

* * *

Ruling Qalala ran through his veins alongside a rich vein of duty. Those two things had always been enough for him in the past, because he was devoted to his country and its people, but without Lucy in his life Tadj couldn't rest, he couldn't think straight, he couldn't sleep, he couldn't function.

After the longest span of loneliness in his life, action was called for. It was long overdue. If such a thing as a eureka moment existed, this was it, Tadj concluded as he slammed down the lid on the latest stack of royal papers. The most important document of all wasn't there. Hardly surprising, when it didn't exist yet. Now he knew what he'd lost, and what he stood to lose, he was ready to fight, not just for Qalala, but for Lucy and their unborn child.

Having called an extraordinary meeting of the royal council, he read out the marriage act, and when his twenty-first-century advisors heard the pronouncements of a bygone age, they had to agree with him that changes must be made.

'Do I take it that love is in the air?' Abdullah, his child-hood friend who sat on the council, and who had first shown Lucy around Wolf Fort, asked him with barely concealed excitement when the meeting had concluded.

'It means I will marry a woman of my choice,' he told Abdullah. 'If she'll have me,' he added dryly, with a hint of humility that was wholly unaccustomed.

'Lucy! I knew it!' Abdullah exclaimed, practically dancing on the spot with excitement. 'She's a challeng-ing one,' he added as if that were the greatest praise, 'and just what you need.'

Tadj hummed as he strode away to put the change in the law into operation.

* * *

He grunted with impatience as he disembarked his jet. Lucy would be seven months pregnant by now. That was how long it had taken to 'speed along' the change to the law in Qalala. What had she done to him? *Was this love?* The thought hit him like a thunderbolt.

Thankfully, being the Emir of Qalala, as well as one of the richest men in the world, came with advantages, one of which was access to the royal fleet of aircraft as well as a royal yacht, added to which were the lack of formalities confronting him when he landed in a foreign country. His yacht was berthed at King's Dock, and he was soon on his way to join it.

He should never have let Lucy go, and he willed the limousine to travel even faster. Seven months pregnant. Only two months to go. Valuable time in a pregnancy. It wasn't too late for him to share the birth of their child, but they still had to discuss the details of what would happen next, and Lucy had steered every conversation they'd had towards talk of the exhibition she was planning with his team. A child mattered more, to both of them, he was sure. She was still suffering from the damage her stepfather had inflicted, and it was up to him to make a difference, so she could face the future with the happiness she deserved.

He had half expected to find Lucy still working at the laundry. He wasn't disappointed. Ruffled and sleep-deprived, with his collar pulled up against the awful weather, as he peered through the steamed-up window his spirits rose. Serving behind the counter, Lucy was as cheerful as ever as she chatted to customers in her usual friendly way.

Pulling back, he felt the loss of her keenly, as if he

were a child with his nose pressed against the window, viewing a treat he couldn't have, a gift he had forfeited for the sake of Mother Duty. He had to take a moment. Seeing Lucy again wrenched at his heart. There was no one like her, and there never would be. He'd never felt like this before. Laying his heart on the line was new to him. Raw sex and power, together with huge wealth and the mystique of royalty, had always been enough to open any door, but these things didn't mean anything to Lucy. She trod her own path, couldn't be wooed with promises of wealth or position. He would have to dig much deeper than that, or he'd lose her for ever.

The doorbell chimed with irritating optimism as he walked into the shop.

'*Tadj!*' Paling, Lucy gripped the counter.

Horror-struck that the sight of him might harm Lucy or the baby, he was holding her in a second. He should have warned her to expect him. Having plunged over the counter to grab her by the arms in case she fell, he held her in front of him to check she was okay. He could breathe again when the colour returned to her face. 'We have to stop meeting like this,' he murmured, drinking her in with all the fervour of a parched man in the desert.

With a hum, she broke free. The customer had left by now, so they were alone. Lucy had snapped back into work mode, pinning tickets on garments, before handing them through the hatch opening onto the steamy heart of the laundry. She was so graceful, so vulnerable, and desirable. Images collided in his mind of her cool hands on his body, and her soft lips on his mouth. 'Can you take a break any time soon?'

'I break for lunch in half an hour,' she said, glancing at the clock.

His spirits lifted, though he was careful to keep his tone casual. 'May I take you for coffee?'

'In the café where we first met?' she said, staring at him as if seeing him for the first time.

'I'll meet you there,' he confirmed.

'It will be busy at lunchtime,' she called after him as he left the shop. 'Bag a table if you get there first.'

Not the best offer he'd ever received from a woman, but, where Project Wooing was concerned, he thought it a reasonable start.

Lucy was late. Where the hell was she? Was she coming at all? He stared at the door, wondering if he'd been stood up, or if she'd run from him again, to some place where he'd never find her. The thought that he'd been stood up amused him, but if she'd gone—he couldn't even contemplate that, so, ordering another coffee, he told himself to use the time to plan and think. Impatience made that impossible. What use was planning, when Lucy was unpredictable? He had to find a way to pin her down, but he needed her here first... He stared with unblinking attention at the door, as if that could make her appear. She was more precious than he'd realised, which was why he hadn't come here with a better offer, but with the ultimate offer, and one he was confident she couldn't refuse.

If she turned up, that was.

Tadj's arriving at the laundry unannounced had really thrown her. What did he want? Did he think she'd changed her mind about becoming his mistress? She racked her brains to think if there was a single problem where work was concerned, but she couldn't think of one. As she'd thought all along, they could communicate perfectly well over the internet, and plans for the various exhibitions of the Qalalan sapphires were progressing well. Hopefully, he was here to talk about the baby. She longed for a compromise, her heart picking up pace just thinking about Tadj, and discussing with him the most important topic in their lives. The prospect of that was like all her Christmases and birthdays come together. *But* he mustn't think he could rule them as he ruled Qalala.

She hurried to take a shower, and, as she was seven months pregnant, getting dressed meant exchanging one shapeless sack for another. Staring at herself in the mirror brought an image of Tadj into her mind. How could he possibly find her attractive in this condition? And why should she care? Surely that meant he wouldn't want her as his mistress, so that was one hurdle she'd jumped over.

The fact that they hadn't exchanged a single personal word since Lucy had left Qalala was as much her fault as his. She'd thought it better to let things cool down, but that meant he'd missed scans, and hearing the heartbeat of their child. She felt bad about that, but he couldn't walk back into her life and think that nothing had changed. She hadn't been sitting around doing nothing these past few months; if he thought that, he was due a surprise.

Snow flurries were settling on the ground as she prepared to leave. It would soon be Christmas. Before then, she'd stop work and concentrate on getting ready to welcome the baby. Her mother had booked a cruise over the holidays, and Lucy planned to spend the time alone. Several friends had offered alternatives, but enjoying the festivities in the midst of a happy family would only remind her how much she missed Tadj.

Anyway, enough of that, she thought, mashing her lips together to blend in the lip gloss. If only she weren't so pregnant and unwieldy—but she was pregnant, and she was unwieldy, Lucy concluded with a wry smile, so, suck it up!

She strode to the café with her head bowed against the wind. Otherwise, she was in no way bowed, but was striding to this meeting loud and proud. And, instead of a shapeless sack, she had shoehorned her body into a figure-hugging dress she'd been saving for Christmas. She didn't want Tadj to think her weak, just because she was pregnant, and she was proud of her baby bump. Which was just as well, Lucy concluded, catching sight of her reflection in a shop window. There was no hiding her condition now, and why should she? With an Honours accreditation in her back pocket, and the promise of a great career ahead, she was doing okay without Tadj. If he wanted to be part of her life, he would have to...

He would just have to ask, Lucy thought wryly as she reached the café and spotted him waiting inside.

The day was transformed from grey and dismal to something vibrant as Lucy breezed in. Her presence cheered everyone up, and turned every head in the café. She approached the table he'd 'bagged' as instructed, in a flurry of flying scarf and watchful eyes. Her cheap red coat refused to fasten over her baby bump, which made her seem even more vulnerable to him than she had in the shop. The bitter wind had turned the tip of her nose the same colour as her coat, which he found endearing.

Standing, he held out her chair. 'How've you been?' he asked as soon as she was settled.

'Pregnant.' Her gaze was steady and long. 'And busy,' she added, softening her tone. 'Did you see the latest drawings I sent?'

'Not only have I seen them, I've approved them,' he confirmed. His team had agreed that Lucy had a real talent when it came to capturing a person's interest before leading them through the story of a sapphire, from its discovery as a rough, unpolished stone, to a glowing gem that added lustre to some of the world's most beautiful women. 'But that isn't what I'm here to talk about,' he said. 'I want to know about you.'

'Me? I feel fantastic,' she said, 'and very excited about the baby.'

'And ready to talk?'

'I am,' she confirmed.

He wanted her alone so much it was eating him up inside. 'I gather you've taken the rest of the afternoon off?'

'I'm not being awkward,' she said, 'but, no, I haven't. I really need this job, and the money it brings in.'

Fortunately, the waitress chose that moment to arrive with coffee, as well as the slices of toasted cheese he'd ordered, anticipating Lucy's pregnancy craving for food. 'I took the liberty of—'

'Brilliant,' she exclaimed. 'I'm famished. But *you* decided *what* I should eat?' she added, frowning deeply. Then she burst into laughter. 'You should see your face. But, seriously, thank you. I'm hungry all the time, and this does look delicious.'

'Tuck in,' he encouraged.

'It won't make any difference,' she assured him as

she polished off the first piece of toast, wedging the last chunk in with her fist. 'Excuse me while I munch this—the baby eats everything before I get a chance. Or, at least, that's what it feels like,' she said, laughing again.

'Take your time, finish up. Are you sure you're getting enough to eat?' he asked with concern as she devoured every scrap of food on her plate, then picked off the crumbs with the pad of her forefinger.

'Haven't you heard about eating for two?'

'Are you sure you're not eating for a litter?'

They both laughed this time, and it felt as if the sun had just come out.

'Quite sure,' she said. 'I've seen the scans. Just me and one baby.'

Carried away on a wave of euphoria, he insisted, 'I still think you need someone to look after you.'

'Do you now?'

He'd been too fast, he thought as she lost the smile, and he would have to be more measured to stand a chance of winning Lucy's trust. Unfortunately, with Lucy sitting there, smiling her challenging smile, that proved impossible.

'Have you finished? Shall we go?' he pressed, standing up, ready to leave.

'Impatient to the last,' she commented as she stared up at him.

'Remember that clock ticking,' he said.

To his relief, she stood too. 'Where were you thinking of going for this talk? I've only got half an hour before I have to be back at the laundry.'

'My yacht's berthed in the marina.'

'Of course it is…' There was a pause and then she said, 'You're not kidding, are you?'

He shrugged. 'Do I ever?'

'Well, I'm not going on your yacht. I don't have time, or the inclination to risk you sailing away with me still on board.'

He curved a smile. 'Why would I subject myself to that?'

'Fair point,' she conceded. 'So, you're really here to talk about the baby.'

'I really am,' he confirmed. 'And talk about us.'

'There is no us,' she said as he ushered her out of the café. 'And I haven't changed my mind,' she added the moment the door to the busy café closed behind them. 'I won't agree to becoming your mistress,' she informed him. 'And I can't be late back, because they're giving me a bit of a send-off tonight—'

'A *send-off*?' he cut in, feeling as if a cold hand were clutching his heart.

'Yes,' Lucy told him matter-of-factly. 'I've decided to set up a small design company—just one team player, namely me. I've managed to save enough from my jobs for the deposit on a small rental property, so I can work from home when the baby arrives. It's all thanks to the start you gave me. News spreads. As soon as the press got wind of the part I'm playing in the tour of the Qa-lalan sapphires, it was all over the news, and the phone never stopped ringing. By the time one becomes two,' she added with a beatific smile as she cupped her hands protectively over the pronounced swell where their baby resided, 'I should be well into my next contract.'

'Bravo,' he said flatly, 'but as you won't be working once the baby arrives I can't see how that's relevant.'

'I'm sorry?' she said.

'Just that,' he said curtly. 'Once our child is born, I'll support you both.'

She stopped dead in the street. 'Maybe I should get back now.'

'No—please,' he added in a more conciliatory tone. 'Just give me half an hour, and I'll explain.'

'I could give you all week, and you still couldn't say anything to change my mind.'

'Hear me out,' he insisted quietly.

She stared at him for a few moments, and then conceded, 'I agreed to make myself available to talk about our baby, and I will.'

'Thank you.'

Available? He seethed in silence as they walked on towards the marina. He had come here to take care of Lucy and the baby, and to do his duty by them, not to have Lucy set the rules.

'I understand how busy you are, so you don't have to do this,' she said. 'You can leave me here.'

'And we'll communicate via our monitor screens? I don't think so,' he said.

'What, then?' she said, throwing her arms wide. 'As you can see, I'm managing very well without you—'

'But you don't have to,' he broke in. 'That's why I'm here. Will you listen to my proposal or not?'

'Not.'

'I beg your pardon?'

She shrugged. 'We need some cooling-off time. I'll be free from around eleven tomorrow.'

'You'll see me now, or not at all,' he insisted as he linked her arm through his.

'You can't just frogmarch me onto your yacht,' Lucy protested as he strode with her towards the marina. 'I have my own life, and free will.' Steel gates swung open at his approach. 'No, Tadj,' she said firmly, pulling back.

Feelings roared inside him, and for a moment he felt like a youth again who'd been played. 'Must we do this in the middle of the street?'

'No,' Lucy said in a maddeningly reasonable tone. 'We can meet again at eleven o'clock tomorrow, when we've both had chance to calm down.'

CHAPTER FIFTEEN

TADJ WAS GRIM-FACED as he returned the salute of his officers as he boarded his yacht. Events had not unfolded as he had anticipated.

This was Lucy, so why expect them to?

The past with all its uncertainties was in his face again, thanks to a woman who had done nothing to deserve his disapproval. In fact, the opposite was true. Rather than wait for him to save the day, Lucy had continued to build a successful future for herself and her child. It was the surprise element of the rain check that got under his skin.

Examining his conscience, he found a few gaps. Had he been completely open with her? Hadn't he filled her in on what he'd been doing? A word or two would have sufficed—would have changed everything between them. Had he expected Lucy to blithely go along with whatever he decided? When had she ever done that? Seething with impatience to see her again, he glanced at his watch. The countdown to tomorrow had begun.

Had she gone too far turning Tadj down? Would she even see him again? Lucy wondered as she got ready for the party. He was the Emir of Qalala, after all, not the guy in the café who'd taken whatever she'd thrown at him in the spirit it was intended. They'd both changed, and no wonder Tadj had lost his sense of humour. She'd had no idea on that first encounter what a rigidly structured life the ruler of a powerful country was forced to lead. Surely Tadj had earned some downtime? No one could ever accuse him of short-changing Qalala. Perhaps it was time to allow the people of Qalala to do something for him. Freeing him to be happy would be a start, and the country could only benefit. No slave of duty could ever give their best, in Lucy's opinion, and she was sad to think Tadj couldn't love where he chose, or enjoy the freedoms she enjoyed. It was duty first, duty always for the Emir of Qalala, she reflected, putting on a sunny face as she came down the stairs and her friends gathered round. They were keen to find out what had happened when she met up with Tadj. There were no secrets in the workplace.

'I didn't want to miss this,' she said honestly, 'so we're meeting again tomorrow morning.'

'You blew out the Emir of Qalala for the chance to be with us?' one of her friends demanded with amazement.

'I wouldn't miss this for the world.'

That same friend looked at her with concern, and then someone else changed the mood as she exclaimed, 'Lucy—Lucy—look at all the gifts for the baby. Can we start to open them now?'

'You shouldn't have spent your money on me,' Lucy exclaimed as she confronted the mountain of carefully wrapped gifts. 'You've gone to far too much trouble.'

'No more than you deserve,' Miss Francine chimed in firmly. 'You're always doing things for us, and now it's our turn to make a fuss of you.'

Excited exclamations greeted the revelation of each

new gift, many of which were painstakingly home-made. She would rather have these genuine tokens of love than all the sapphires in the world, Lucy concluded as she unwrapped them. If only Tadj could understand that.

He had never been more certain that something was right, or that it could slip through his fingers so easily. Losing Lucy was unthinkable. It would spell disaster for them and for their child. She had every quality he'd been searching for in a queen. The only surprise was that he, with his reputation for decisive action, had remained blinkered for so long. Lucy's strength and determination set her apart from the so-called *suitable* princesses. With her natural flair and warmth, she was everything he could wish for. If this were a straightforward business deal, he would have secured her long before now. But this wasn't a straightforward business deal.

Inside his suite on board his yacht the *Blue Stone*, he studied the priceless sapphire in his hand. Everything hinged on his next move. Tucking the precious gemstone into the back pocket of his jeans, he railed at the thought that he must wait. If he attempted to bounce Lucy into a decision, she'd bounce the other way. As a lover his credentials were sound; as a man in love, he had so far proved to be pretty useless. It was time to sort that out.

So, this was it, Lucy thought. Still glowing from the party her friends had thrown for her the previous night, she'd slept fitfully, waking long before dawn had brightened her bedsit. And then she'd spent ages pacing and fretting, instead of getting ready to meet Tadj. She should have drawn up a list—an agenda—something he would understand. Frowning as she chewed her lip worriedly, she stared out of the window at the distant shape of the *Blue Stone*, which was floating like a slumbering leviathan at anchor just a few hundred yards away. It was almost eleven o'clock on a cold grey winter's morning. Even the sky looked like a sheet of ice. Wrapping up warmly would do nothing to protect her heart, she mused wryly as she wound a scarf around her neck. Even her much vaunted common sense couldn't help when Tadj was in the frame. She loved him unconditionally, which made her more vulnerable than she would like. Grabbing her cross-shoulder bag, she checked the contents before leaving the room.

'Call me stupid,' she told her friends and Miss Francine as they gathered around her to wish her well, 'but I'm really excited at the thought of seeing him again.'

'Not stupid,' Miss Francine insisted as she brought Lucy into her arms for a hug. 'A woman in love could never be called stupid in my book.'

Lucy's friends chipped in with their own raucous suggestions, drowning out Miss Francine as Lucy gave her elderly friend an extra hug. 'We make our own luck,' she said as she made her way to the door. 'So I'd better get out there, and get busy making some.'

'Just don't let him walk roughshod over you,' a friend called out.

'Who's going to protect the Emir?' Miss Francine countered.

There was no protection against love, Lucy thought as she said goodbye to her friends and left the shop.

As she fell beneath the shadow of the *Blue Stone*, she could see Tadj waiting out on deck. Her heart went crazy, but when he jogged down the companionway to greet her, they exchanged nothing more than polite kisses on both cheeks. Her lips still tingled from contact with his warm, firm skin, and from the lightest rasp of his stubble. She missed the wildness of their passion, and knew that might never return. Even if it had, she reflected with amusement, on this huge vessel surrounded by officers in crisp whites, it would hardly be appropriate to greet the Emir of Qalala with anything but discretion and reserve. Well, maybe a little more than that, she conceded as she stared deep into Tadj's unreadable eyes. She wouldn't have cared who was watching if things had been normal between them.

'Welcome on board the *Blue Stone*,' the Emir of Qalala intoned stiffly. 'After you,' he invited politely.

So it was going to be formality all the way, Lucy thought with a heavy heart. Once inside the *Blue Stone*, her disappointment was soon forgotten.

'Goodness, this is amazing,' she exclaimed. Talk about leaving one world behind and entering another. This *was* amazing. She felt shabby in contrast to her surroundings. Everything was pristine and polished. 'I thought your friend Sheikh Khalid's yacht was amazing, but this is—'

'Doubly amazing?' Tadj supplied.

'Yes,' she said, staring directly into his eyes. Was that a hint of humour? Was Tadj back?

'Are you expecting someone?' she asked as they walked deeper into the floating palace. Maybe he was expecting more guests, she thought, taking in all the fabulous floral displays dressing the grand salon. It was a blow to think he might cut their meeting short. 'Unless this is just how the other half lives?' she suggested.

'It could be how you live,' he said.

'I believe we've already had that discussion.'

'I believe we have,' he agreed with a look that reduced her to a lustful crisp.

She barely had chance to register this fact before Tadj yanked her hard against his body. 'I'm mad to have waited so long,' he said.

'To shanghai me?' she demanded, shivering with excitement and dread.

Stepping back, Tadj lifted up his hands. She felt the loss of him immediately. He knew what he was doing. Nothing Tadj did was ever unintentional.

'Sit,' he invited in a voice she couldn't read.

'Better not—pregnancy? I might fall asleep.'

'How flattering,' he commented with the lift of one brow.

The tension between them was unsustainable, Lucy thought as she quickly explained, 'I just tire easily.'

'And must be hungry, I'm guessing.'

Before she could answer this, he tugged a bell pull on the wall. 'And then a siesta, I think.'

'Oh, no,' Lucy protested. 'I'm not staying that long.'

A discreet knock on the door heralded the arrival of a parade of stewards, carrying all sorts of tempting delicacies into the room. And she was starving.

Somehow eating made everything seem normal again, and the tension between them evaporated, leaving them free to discuss the future of their child. Tadj was keen that both cultures were given equal weight, and that they must both have a say in every decision.

'A say?' Lucy queried, worrying that her opinion might carry no weight. Tadj held all the financial cards, making it impossible for her to fight him through the courts.

'Don't look for trouble,' he warned. 'You're the child's

mother, so of course your views will be listened to and implemented if we agree they're beneficial. And, yes, I did use the word *we*,' he confirmed.

This was a massive adjustment for Tadj, and he hadn't finished surprising her yet. 'What's this?' she asked as he handed her a document.

'Read it and you'll see.'

Tadj would uphold Lucy's right to independence in deciding how best to mother her child. 'You're giving up all your rights,' she said.

'Because I trust you,' he stated frankly.

Her heart clenched tight, but she had to be sure of his motives. 'Does this mean you don't want the responsibility?'

'Quite the opposite. I intend to take a full part in the upbringing of our child, but it's important that you feel secure. You mustn't ever feel threatened at any point. Carry on working for as long as you feel able to—do everything that makes you *you*.'

She didn't need anyone to tell her what this must have cost Tadj in time and effort when it came to changing things in Qalala, or how far he'd come in personal terms.

'I just have one question,' he said. 'Do you trust me?'

This was such an important moment, crucial for Tadj, yet an image chose this moment to pop unhelpfully into her head. She had never imagined making such a vital pledge while heavily pregnant with grease around her mouth, having scoffed every bit of food in sight.

'Lucy...?'

Turning away, she mopped her mouth with a napkin, which gave her chance to draw a deep, steadying breath. 'Yes, I trust you,' she said with absolute certainty. 'I trust you with my life. And, more importantly, with the life of our child.'

'Then, I have something to say.'

He sounded so formal now, more like the Emir than Tadj.

'Can you say it after that siesta you mentioned?'

Tadj seemed surprised. 'I'm not sure I can wait.'

She stared into his face and a quiver of arousal ran through her. 'You could join me.'

'If that's what you want.'

He sounded so stern, but as he picked up her bag and coat she saw a look in his eyes she recognised. 'It is what I want. We could share the bed?'

Tadj threw her a look that sent her senses into freefall. 'How accommodating you can be.'

'When the offer promises so much, why would I hesitate?'

'Good news for me,' he said dryly.

He was back. The man she'd fallen in love with was back. 'What was it you wanted to say to me?' she remembered as they left the room.

'It can wait,' he said, and, linking their fingers, he led her to his suite.

He'd barely shut the door, when he brought her into his arms and kissed her. 'Marry me,' he said while she was still gasping for breath.

'Are you serious?' Lucy exclaimed, taken completely by surprise.

'What do you think this is?' Tadj growled as he backed her towards the bed.

'Evidence that you're pleased to see me after all?'

He laughed, and with a new freedom, she thought as he demanded, 'Can you be serious for a moment?'

'If I must.'

'I think you must.'

'Marry me, and all this—' he glanced around '—will be yours.'

'I don't want anything but you.'

But he didn't appear to hear her. 'The *Blue Stone* is only one of many assets I own across the world—take your pick.'

I choose you, she thought. The rest is unnecessary. I don't need it. The type of riches he was describing were better suited to a princess, or an heiress, not a working single mother with no time on her hands to appreciate them. They should belong to a woman with expectations, and all Lucy wanted was love.

'I'm sorry. I can't marry you,' she said. 'I can't allow you to do this, when we both know I bring nothing to Qalala's benefit.'

'You bring everything,' Tadj argued fiercely. 'You're everything I've ever wanted and everything Qalala needs.' Cupping her face in his hands, he stared deep into her eyes. 'I'm bringing Qalala into the modern age, and with you at my side I can achieve that faster. And I know you don't expect an easy ride.'

'I never have,' she said. 'But marriage is a step too far. You don't need to feel sorry for me.'

'Sorry for you?' he said. 'I know what you're capable of, which is why I'm asking you to be my wife.'

Lucy shook her head. 'I love you too much to see you sacrifice everything for me.'

'I don't have to. If you love me, it's enough.' Tadj went on to explain how the constitution of Qalala had been amended to allow the Emir to marry a wife of his choosing, rather than accept a bride chosen by commit-tee. 'You do love me?' he confirmed.

'More than life itself,' Lucy admitted with her cus-tomary bluntness.

They stared at each other, and then Tadj said, 'So you'll marry me.'

'Is that any way to ask?'

The tension broke and they laughed.

'Excuse me, my lady,' he said, making her a mock bow. But as he got down on one knee, he made a fatal error. 'As our marriage is already arranged, I should, I suppose, ask you formally.'

'What?' Lucy exclaimed, in no mood to hear any-thing more. 'If our marriage is arranged, you'd better unarrange it.'

'And have our child raised out of wedlock? Surely, you understand I can't allow that.'

'I don't see that it makes any difference at all,' Lucy said as he sprang up. 'Our child will be brought up with love—what else matters? A child needs to feel loved, and secure and happy. Do you think it cares about a piece of paper?'

'A royal child will be under scrutiny.'

'True, but you could have asked me first—warned me that plans for our wedding were already under way. It is usual.'

'Do you expect me to be patient now?'

'You?' she queried with a glimmer of grim humour. 'No. But I do expect you to grant me an equal say over everything we do. That is what you promised.'

He should have paced things differently, given Lucy more warning and a better build-up to his proposal. He'd be there for her and their child whatever her answer now.

But her answer had to be in the affirmative 'This *is* the best,' he said. 'How can it be otherwise? Do you propose to live on the opposite side of the world?'

'So your concern for appearances has driven this proposal?' she exclaimed. 'Silly me, when I thought you were in love and being romantic.'

'I am being romantic,' he blazed, or he was doing his best, anyway. 'What about you and me? Don't we deserve happiness?'

'No one deserves happiness,' she countered hotly. 'It has to be earned. And never at the expense of anyone else.'

'You can play the saint all you want,' he exploded, 'but please don't expect me to do the same!'

Frustration was hammering at his brain and Lucy was equally heated. Grabbing him, she wrestled hard, rubbing her body against his in her passion. If this was fate, he was destined to get the best workout every single day of his life.

Fate had thrown them together, and now demanded action, Lucy thought as she ripped at Tadj's clothes.

'Slow—careful—don't forget your condition,' he insisted as she battled to get him naked.

'I haven't forgotten anything!' she flared. Pregnancy had made her mad for sex, mad for him. Knowing pleasure was only a few deep thrusts away made her fiercer than ever.

'No,' Tadj said firmly. Standing back, he refastened his jeans. 'Not here like this...'

Hormones snapping left her ready to scream he couldn't frustrate her like this, but, scooping her up, he carried her to the bed. 'Now,' he murmured with that annoying half-smile of his tugging at one corner of his mouth. 'Where were we?'

Stripping her efficiently, he positioned and controlled her buttocks with his big, slightly roughened hands, and then took her with the utmost care, but with the utmost thoroughness too, she was happy to report. One deep thrust with a sensational massaging motion of his hips at the end of it was all it took to tip her over the edge into screaming pleasure. While she responded in time to each powerful spasm, Tadj continued to move steadily, ensuring the next release was upon her before the first had even ended.

'So, what's your answer to my proposal?' he demanded the moment she was quiet.

'It hasn't changed,' she said, dragging in some much-needed air. 'You belong to Qalala and I belong here—well, as close as damn it when I move.'

'Move?' Tadj demanded. 'Move where?' Releasing her, and withdrawing, he swung her around. Horns locked, they glared at each other, until something changed in Tadj's eyes. Had he finally accepted the gulf between them was too wide?

She should have known better. Lifting her, he carried her into the bathroom, where, stripping off, he switched on the shower. 'I need an answer, Lucy.'

His eyes were black, and his body was magnificent. And she, unusually, was lost for words, so she shrugged. 'I'm moving out of my bedsit,' she managed finally. 'It's too small…' She gasped as he backed her into the shower. Turning her to face the wall, he nudged her legs apart with his, and made sure that this was the very best shower she'd ever experienced.

CHAPTER SIXTEEN

MUCH LATER, WHEN they lay entwined on Tadj's bed, Lucy turned her head to say, 'Even after everything you've told me about the changes in the constitution of Qalala, I can't marry you.'

'Because?' Tadj queried, his voice made husky by the exertions of love.

'I can't because I'm not equipped to be the wife of an emir.'

'I beg to differ,' he said, reaching for her. 'I'd say you were extremely well equipped. And as for your use of the word *can't*? It doesn't suit you. I've never known you to give up so easily.'

'You've never known me in love before,' Lucy confessed. 'I can't agree to anything I think might hurt you.'

'You'll hurt me if you don't marry me. Who else will I have to argue with?'

Swinging her beneath him before she could answer, he pinned her hands above her head in one big fist. Teasing her stubborn lips apart, he kissed her, and remained looming over her. 'You're everything to me,' he said bluntly. 'You don't hurt me. You challenge me, and I need that. You opened my eyes to more possibilities for Qalala. The country needs you more than it needs my money.'

'As I do,' she said. 'So stop offering me castles and country homes, when all I want is your heart.'

'You've got it,' Tadj said fiercely. 'My people need love, and that's what you give them.'

'How do I do that?'

'By being you. You make people happy. I've seen you in action, remember?'

'At the party in the mountains?'

'Everywhere. People trust you—as I do,' Tadj admitted.

'And is this how you intend to persuade me?' she demanded as he rasped his stubble against her neck.

'Yes.' And showing no sign of remorse, let alone tiring, Tadj took her again.

Tightening her muscles around him, she evened things up, bringing him to a thundering climax within…um, maybe half an hour. A long time later when her limbs were so heavy with contentment she could barely move, Tadj asked her to marry him again.

'I haven't changed my mind. You've made a good case, bringing Qalala into the modern world, and raising our family together, but—'

'But nothing,' he said. 'We belong together. And if you want me to prove it again…'

'You're not exhausted?'

'Should I be?' Binding her close in his arms, he said, 'Now it's your turn to listen to me. Neither of us has been idle while we've been apart, and I've made the choice of my bride.'

'Do I have a say in this, or is that a command, Your Majesty?'

'Well, it isn't a humble request,' Tadj admitted.

'I imagine not,' Lucy agreed dryly. 'That would be so unlike you. But I do have one request.'

'Name it.'

'I get to organise my own wedding.'

'Granted,' he said, acting stern. 'Though the royal ceremony—'

'Will require expert input,' she agreed. 'That's where you come in.'

'Don't tempt me. Oh, okay,' Tadj conceded. 'I'm tempted…'

There was quite a lengthy interlude before they got back to talking business. 'Be warned, you'll be taking on a lifetime of duty,' he said.

'Don't forget love,' Lucy added. 'Right now my heart feels ready to explode.'

'Indigestion?' Tadj queried.

'Love,' Lucy said firmly, thinking how sexy Tadj looked when he narrowed his eyes like that. 'Love,' she repeated softly, knowing she would stand by this man through thick and thin.

'I ask nothing more of you,' he said.

'Will you marry me for love?' she asked softly.

'Is that a proposal?' Tadj asked, eyes glinting with amusement as he tipped his head to one side.

'Could be…'

'I have something for you,' he said when he'd kissed her.

'What a coincidence,' Lucy replied. 'I have something for you.'

'Show me,' Tadj insisted.

Slipping out of bed, she grabbed a throw, and, padding across the bedroom, she entered the stateroom where Tadj had left her bag.

'What's this?' he asked when she returned and handed him an envelope.

'Open it and see…'

Tadj stilled as he recognised the significance of the black and white image in his hand. 'It's your baby…our baby,' Lucy explained.

'And this is the only time you'll ever see me cry,' Tadj assured her.

'Are you pleased?' She came to join him on the bed.

'You should have warned me,' he said.

'I don't think anything can prepare you for that,' Lucy murmured as she stared over his shoulder at the blurry image of their unborn child.

Tadj couldn't tear his gaze away from it, but finally he looked up. 'You've made me the happiest man on earth,' he murmured. 'I said I had something for you, but it seems worthless compared to this.'

Holding the fragile image to his hard-muscled chest, as if he couldn't bear to part with it, he reached for a small velvet box in the drawer in the nightstand.

Guessing what it might be, Lucy protested, 'But I really don't need anything else, when I've got you, and our child.'

'Which is a hell of a lot more than you must have expected when you walked into that café that day.'

Lucy's heart overflowed with love as Tadj stole another glance at the black and white image. Placing it on the nightstand, he brought her into his arms. 'I think we both got a lot more than we bargained for that day.'

And every day from now on, Lucy thought as Tadj teased her lips apart and kissed her again.

'No. Absolutely not. I can't accept this!' Lucy protested many hours later, when they had showered and dressed, and Tadj's arms were loosely linked around her waist as they stared out across the winter scene on the marina. He had just slipped the most amazing ring onto her finger.

'You must,' he insisted as she stared in disbelief at the fabulous lustrous blue sapphire with its circle of flashing diamonds. 'If you don't, the world will think the Qalalan sapphires aren't good enough for my bride.'

'What a line,' she said. 'If you think you can convince me.'

'I can and I will,' Tadj assured her.

The ring was very beautiful—stunning, in fact, Lucy mused as she stared into its rich blue heart. Qalalan sapphires were as blue as the ocean on a sunny day, and the diamonds around its blue depths sparkled like sunlight on the waves.

'I really can't,' she insisted. 'This ring is the centrepiece of the touring exhibition. We open on Valentine's Day in London, remember?'

'How clever of you to have this most amazing sapphire and diamond engagement ring as the highlight of the tour,' Tadj commented straight-faced.

'You don't even sound surprised,' Lucy noted with suspicion.

'I'm not. Clever of my craftsmen to ask you to try it on, don't you think?'

'You—'

'I intend to stay one step ahead of you,' he informed her with a wicked grin.

'I wish you joy of that.'

'Something tells me I'm going to need it,' Tadj agreed.

'The ring stays with the exhibition,' Lucy insisted. 'And I won't change my mind,' she added as Tadj sank to underhand tactics when he rasped his sharp black stubble against her neck.

'I designed the ring for you,' he explained. 'There isn't another like it in the world. We'll choose something else to take centre stage in the exhibition…something huge and heart-shaped in celebration of Valentine's Day, and far too cheesy for you.'

'You arranged this all along, didn't you?' Lucy accused softly.

'Guilty as charged,' Tadj admitted, lips pressing down as he gave a casual shrug.

'Is it always going to be like this?' Lucy demanded with a mock warning frown.

'I certainly hope so.'

Tadj's mouth had curved in an irresistible grin that warned Lucy to be on her guard. 'I will definitely need to keep my wits about me,' she said, trying to sound stern.

'But not your clothes, I hope…'

It was only a short stride for a strong man to carry his bride-to-be to the bedroom.

EPILOGUE

LUCY AND TADJ'S first wedding ceremony had been a small, intimate ceremony at King's Dock on board the *Blue Stone*. They had delayed their marriage until the warmer, more optimistic days of spring had allowed everyone they were close to to attend, including Lucy's mother, who had been home from her cruise and had looked at least ten years younger. The day had been everything Lucy had ever dreamed of, as well as a thrill for Miss Francine, whose laundry had received a complete overhaul, thanks to Tadj's generosity. Miss Francine had taken a full part in the ceremony as one of Lucy's maids of honour, and had been most ably escorted by Tadj's courtly aide, Abdullah.

On that first wedding day Miss Francine had fussed over Lucy's simple wedding gown, until Lucy had been sure it would be steamed out of existence. Much the same was happening today with a much grander dress, as Lucy and her friends and family prepared for the big public ceremony in Qalala. The youngest, and most important bridesmaid, was Lottie, as Princess Charlotte was known. A Christmas Day baby, Lottie had been delivered by Tadj, when she'd proved as impatient as her father. A turkey dinner would never be the same again, Lucy reflected with loving amusement as her mother held up Lottie for a kiss.

The streets of Qalala were packed with locals and visitors from across the world. Who could resist what had been dubbed 'the love match of the century'? Lucy thought, smiling as she counted the minutes until she'd see Tadj. And then she did see him—reflected in her mirror. 'You're not supposed to be here,' she scolded as he strode into the room.

Dismissing everyone, he embraced his wife. 'You didn't expect me to wait, did you?'

'No,' Lucy admitted, thinking what a magnificent sight he was in his robes of state.

'You're not supposed to be so beautiful,' he teasingly complained, drawing her into his arms. 'How am I supposed to resist you?'

'You're not,' she said. 'What's this?' she added as he handed over an official-looking sheaf of documents.

'Your next commission,' he said. 'I intend to keep you working. My fellow Sapphire Sheikhs are jealous of my exhibition, and have asked if you would arrange something similar for them. You'll be kept busy,' he promised. 'Though, not too busy…'

'Tadj,' she exclaimed, guessing that his intentions were far from honourable. 'In a tiara and wedding dress?'

'If that's what it takes,' he said with a shrug. 'Though, please try not to move, or your crown might drop off…'

'I hope you're joking?'

'Joke when I make love to my wife?'

Some time later, Lucy was forced to take a quick dip in the bath, complete with crown, before Tadj helped her to dress again in the fabulous gown he'd insisted on buying for her in Paris on one of their many trips.

'You look beautiful,' Lucy's mother breathed, standing back to admire the daughter she knew would take care of her wherever she lived.

'More than beautiful,' Miss Francine added.

Tadj could only agree with everyone's opinion of his stunning bride, and as Lucy walked towards him on her mother's arm, down the long aisle that led to their future, he knew without doubt that he was the luckiest man on earth.

'It seems like only yesterday that we were sitting across a Formica table, teasing each other,' Lucy told him, long after the wedding feast had ended, and they were alone at last in Tadj's apartment at the royal palace.

'What's changed?' he growled as he dragged her close. 'All this—' he glanced around at the formal gilding and decoration, the marble pillars stretching up to colourful frescoes on a vaulted roof above the royal four-poster bed '—is just the icing on the cake.'

'Are you suggesting I'm crumby?'

'Anything but,' he said, laughing as he removed her tiara and necklace.

In just her high-heeled white satin shoes and a skimpy lace basque, with fine silk stockings, Lucy had to ask the obvious question. 'Would you like me to order coffee to go with your cake?'

'Why waste time?' Tadj demanded as she wriggled out of the rest of her clothes.

There were occasions when it felt good to assert her authority, and others times she was quite happy to let Tadj do all the work…and this was one of those times.

'I love you,' Tadj whispered later, much later, when she was sated and they were snuggled up in bed.

'And I love you,' she whispered, staring deep into his eyes.

'For ever,' Tadj murmured.

'Not long enough,' Lucy complained in a groggy, smiling whisper against his mouth.

'My wife.'

'My husband.'

'My world.'

* * * * *

COMING SOON!

We really hope you enjoyed reading this book. If you're looking for more romance, be sure to head to the shops when new books are available on

Thursday 13th December

To see which titles are coming soon, please visit **millsandboon.co.uk**

MILLS & BOON

MILLS & BOON

Coming next month

THE SECRET KEPT FROM THE ITALIAN
Kate Hewitt

'Maisie.'

Antonio looked up at the sound of her name on another man's lips. The man was standing by the entrance to the hotel, a smile on his face as he held out his arms. Slowly Antonio turned and saw Maisie walking towards the man, a tremulous smile curving her lush lips, a baby nestled in her arms.

A baby.

Antonio stared as the man took the baby from her, cuddling the little bundle as he cooed down at it.

'Hey, sweetie.'

Jealousy fired through Antonio, although he couldn't even say why. So Maisie had moved on, found a boyfriend or husband, and had a baby pretty darn quick. That was fine. Of course it was. Except...

They'd spent the night together a year ago, and although Antonio wasn't an expert on babies by any means, the child nestled in the man's arms looked to be at least a few months old. Which meant...

Either Maisie had been pregnant when she'd slept with him, or had fallen pregnant immediately after. Or, he realised with a sickening rush, had become pregnant by him.

He hadn't used birth control. He'd been too drunk and emotional even to think of it at the time, and later he'd assumed Maisie must have been on the pill, since she hadn't seemed concerned. But now he remembered how she'd come to see him—how many weeks later? Two, three? She'd wanted to talk to him. She'd looked distraught. What if she'd been pregnant?

Why had he not considered such a possibility? Antonio retrained his shocked gaze on the man and baby, only to realise they'd already gone. Maisie had turned around and was walking back towards the ballroom, and presumably her waitressing duties. And his child might have just been hustled out of the door.

'Maisie.' His voice came out in a bark of command, and Maisie turned, her jade-green eyes widening as she caught sight of him. Then her face drained of colour, so quickly and dramatically that Antonio felt another rush of conviction. Why would she react like that if the child wasn't his?

'What are you doing here?' she asked in a low voice.

'I'm a guest at the dinner.'

'Yes, but…what do you want from me, Antonio?' She looked wretched, and more than once her gaze darted towards the doors and then back again.

'Let's talk in private.'

'You weren't so interested in doing that the last time we met,' Maisie snapped, summoning some spirit.

'Yes, I know, but things are different now.'

'They're different for me too.' She took a step backwards, her chin raised at a proud, determined angle. 'You didn't want to know me a year ago, Antonio, and now I don't want to know you. Doesn't feel very good, does it?' She gave a hollow laugh.

'This is not the time to be petty,' Antonio returned evenly. 'We need to talk.'

'No, we don't—'

'Maisie.' He cut her off, making her flinch. 'Is the baby mine?'

Continue reading
THE SECRET KEPT FROM THE ITALIAN
Kate Hewitt

Available next month
www.millsandboon.co.uk

LET'S TALK
Romance

For exclusive extracts, competitions
and special offers, find us online:

 facebook.com/millsandboon

@millsandboonuk

@millsandboon

Or get in touch on 0844 844 1351*

For all the latest titles coming soon, visit
millsandboon.co.uk/nextmonth